QUARTET

QUARTET

new voices from South Africa

ALEX LA GUMA/ JAMES MATTHEWS

ALF WANNENBURGH/ RICHARD RIVE

COMPILED AND EDITED BY RICHARD RIVE

Crown Publishers, Inc., New York

Printed in the United States of America

for

ZEKE MPHAHLELE

*in admiration and regard for his work for
literature on the African Continent in
general and for his, and our, country,
South Africa, in particular.*

ACKNOWLEDGMENTS

Adelphi Literary Review for Echoes. *African Songs* for Rain, Resurrection, Strike. No Room at Solitaire. *Africa South* for Azikwelwa, Out of Darkness. *Africa Berattar* for The Park, Out of Darkness, Resurrection. *Afrika Kertoo* for The Park, Out of Darkness, Resurrection. *Azikwelwa* for The Party, Azikwelwa, The Park, The Portable Radio. *Atlantis* for Resurrection. *Drum* for Resurrection. *Contrast* for Rain. *Fighting Talk* for Slipper Satin, A Glass of Wine, *Black Orpheus* for Awendgesang, Echoes, Slipper Satin, A Glass of Wine. *New African Echoes* for The Snake Pit, *New Age* for Nocturne, Resurrection. *Negro Digest* for Echoes, Strike. *Transition* for Nocturne, The Park, Debut, Resurrection.

CONTENTS

FOUR SPLENDID VOICES

by Alan Paton

Our South African literature in English flourishes in a truly indigenous climate, years of plenty followed by years of drought. Then the rain comes again, and the veld is riotous with flowers. The flowering of 1963 is called *Quartet,* a collection of sixteen stories from four writers: Alex La Guma, James Matthews, Richard Rive, and Alf Wannenburgh. We have never had an anthology like this one, nor one better named. These four voices sing perfectly together.

Of course the members of quartet must all sing the same song. They have different parts and their voices have different qualities, but the song is the same. It has many sub themes, but only one grand theme: South Africa,

11

with all its harshness and sadness and tenderness and richness. That is the same as saying that its grand theme is life, life as it is and moves and throbs in South Africa. One can narrow it down further, and say that the theme is largely life as it is and moves and throbs in Cape Town, our mother city. This does not make *Quartet* restricted and parochial; on the contrary it defines it, making it clear-cut and universal. *Quartet* has a clean shape and meaning; Richard Rive did his editing well.

I remember that Uys Krige, our only Afrikaner troubadour, once said that the South African writer need not write about the country's racial and political situation, that he could write the love idyll of a boy and girl in Basutoland, lost in the mountains and each other. Well, of course he could. But of these sixteen stories in *Quartet,* twelve at least deal directly with this very situation. These writers don't preach or harangue or tell you what would be nicer. They tell stories about South Africa. They tell about life as they see it. This attempt to tell is called art. If it succeeds, it's called good art. *Quartet* succeeds.

The rules of writing and story-telling are inexorable. If you break them, your writing fails, your story isn't good. The inexorable rule is that you must put your story first, not your politics or religion or your anger about the Group Areas Act. This does not mean that your politics or your religion or your anger must be left out of your story. On the contrary, they inform the story, and give it color and warmth and fire. But they must never usurp the place of the prime motive, which is to tell a story.

The writers of *Quartet* know these rules well. That is remarkable, for three of them at least must daily suffer many kinds of discrimination. But they are not primarily telling of discrimination, they are telling of life; and because they are primarily telling of life, they inevitably tell about discrimination. It is to my mind significant that it is always white people who resent stories about our racial situation. It is always a white reviewer who says, "Here is that refreshing thing, a story which does not deal with the racial situation." What has that got to do with it? The important thing is, is it a good story? If it is, then it doesn't matter what it deals with. But if you are not white, it is ten to one that your story will deal with the racial situation, because that is your life.

The future of the English language, and therefore of South Africans writing in English, causes many English-speaking people anxiety, and not without reason. Some English-speaking people are already preparing their children for Afrikanerization, not by teaching them Afrikaans, but by recommending to them race theories that have traditionally always been expressed in Afrikaans. Here in *Quartet* is contrary evidence, namely that writers whom one might have expected to write in Afrikaans tell their harsh and tender stories in English—and good English too, full of directness and vigor. Some day we may expect South African writers of Indian descent to do the same, to give us stories of Durban to match these stories of Cape Town. Our literature in English grows slowly, but it seems to be true that more and more South Africans want to write about South African life. The Afrikaner writer has always suffered from the inhibitions that exclusive nationalism causes in creative artists, and it may be that these inhibitions are beginning to affect English-speaking writers too. They certainly do not affect the writers of *Quartet*. Their anthology is a milestone in the history of South African literature.

Without Justice

While there is a lower class, I am in it.
While there is a criminal element, I am of it.
While there is a soul in jail, I am not free.
—EUGENE V. DEBS

STRIKE
by *Richard Rive*

TWENTY-SEVENTH MAY. Stay at home call by Action Council on eve of South African Republic. Pan African Congress in united front abroad backs demonstrations. Mandela's appeal. Coloreds, Indians back African action.

Two men sweating at a duplicating machine.
"Get cracking! Pamphlets for Bernie."
"Bernie's pamphlets coming up. What about Athlone?"
"Athlone ready. Ten thousand coming up."
"We need three extra workers at Athlone."
"And one in Claremont. Jim's been arrested."
"When they pick him up?"
"Last night. Cops caught him putting up strike notices."
"Where's he now?"

"Claremont Police Station. Mervyn's trying for bail."

"Hope he gets it."

"Athlone coming up. Fifteen thousand for Cape Town Central."

"Hell, that'll take some counting."

"Gotta have it ready by tonight."

"New shift working in Cape Town?"

"No. Same five, plus eight students."

"Hope all this is not for nothing. Think they'll come out?"

"Who?"

"The workers."

"They should. But the colored workers are a problem."

"Africans dependable?"

"They should be after the last time."

"You know, of course, P.A.C. will come out against us."

"I don't think that's any problem."

"Could be serious. They have strong support in the Cape."

"Not quite our problem at the moment. We have fifteen thousand pamphlets to count."

"Right. Let's get stuck into Cape Town Central."

"Okay."

There is something about Upper Long Street that is different from the lower half. It is clean and dirty, modern and old-fashioned, plastic and enamel, with just a touch

18

of crinoline and sedan chair. It is moral and immoral.
Its shops are respectable, its lanes notorious. It contains
bank managers and clerks, whores and pimps. Mosques
and churches. Englishmen, Afrikaners, coloreds, Moslems,
Africans, Jews, gentiles, Germans, Greeks, Italians. It is
South African and un-South African. The lower half is
sophisticated and pretentious, the upper half vulgar and
unpretentious.

Boston Cloete and Lennie Damons turned into it from
Wale Street.

"We're nearing the bookshop now. It's not far to go.
Only two blocks further," Boston said.

"I hope so. Do you think he'll have it ready?"

"Who?"

"Katzen."

"I suppose so. I don't know the man."

"Apparently he's a strong sympathizer, that's why he's
helping to distribute pamphlets."

"Who's supposed to drop them?"

"Joel."

"This looks like the shop."

Boston spoke with a slightly affected accent that made
people look at him twice in conversation and wonder
where he came from; it offended at first until one became
used to it. His face was dark brown, with heavy bushy
eyebrows and a firm jaw. His hair was black and wavy.
In Durban he could pass for an Indian, only his accent
gave him away. He was soberly dressed except for a brown

19

suede jacket that he hoped gave him a Bohemian touch. Just sufficient to indicate that he wrote short stories. He was in his late twenties, and just starting to put on weight.

He paused outside a dimly lit secondhand bookshop and compared the number on the door with that on the back of an envelope he took from his pocket.

"Yeah, seems like it," Lennie agreed, peering over his shoulder. Lennie was as taciturn as Boston was voluble. He became cynical when aroused. Very dark in complexion, he was often embarrassed when mistaken for African. He didn't like being mistaken for African. His face was round and the skin smooth and healthy. He was an artist, fairly successful, but his portly shape belied the myth of a starving painter. His clothes were neat, but somewhat loud in contrast to his cautious personality. Many thought him arrogant, and he did nothing to counteract his reputation.

"Well, let's go in!" Boston said.

The bookshop was empty except for a bespectacled attendant sitting at a desk in the far corner and a University student leafing through *Teach Yourself Calculus*. It was darker inside after the brilliant glare of Long Street, and it took Boston some time to get accustomed to the light. The University student nodded to the attendant and left. Lennie wandered over to the Africana section.

"May I help you?"

"Well, yes," Boston began hesitantly. "Are you Mr. Katzen?"

"Yes?"

"I'm Cloete. Boston Cloete. I'm supposed to pick up a parcel left for me."

"Oh, yes. It's at the back of the shop. Is that the parcel Joel left?"

"That's it."

"I'll get it for you. Won't be a minute." He disappeared into a back room.

"So?" Lennie asked, raising his eyebrows.

"He seems all right. Wonder if he knows Joel."

"He must."

"Or about the strike pamphlets."

"Possibly."

"Seems a sympathizer. There are few whites nowadays prepared to help."

"I guess so."

Mr. Katzen reappeared with a brown paper parcel tied with string.

"Here we are. Thanks."

"Thanks very much, Mr. Katzen," Boston said, putting it into his empty satchel.

"Haven't I met you before?" the book dealer inquired. He seemed the talkative type. Boston felt he had to get away. He was still suspicious and self-conscious about most whites.

"I don't think so."

"Are you by any means a writer?"

"Well, yes. I try to."

"That's it. I remember your name. I read some of your stuff."

"Yes?"

"I cannot recollect where, but I remember the name distinctly. Boston Cloete. I liked your stories very much."

Boston felt embarrassed. He found compliments gratifying but was never quite sure how to accept them. Lennie watched patiently.

"This is Len Damons."

"Oh, yes, the artist."

"Yes, the artist," Lennie repeated. They shook hands and an uncomfortable pause followed.

"Well, thanks again, Mr. Katzen, we must be off."

"Good luck. And I hope everything works out all right."

They left the dark interior for the bustle and brilliant sunshine outside. It was one of those bright Saturday mornings.

"Wonder if he can be trusted," Boston said.

"Wonder!" Lennie replied.

Vast patrols next week in peninsula. Police chief's reassurance. Peninsula is prepared for possible strike. Undeclared state of emergency begins. The people demand a national convention.

He found his own relations hardest to convince. Bleary-eyed from lack of sleep. Arguing, canvassing, discussing.

"But what do you want us to do?"

"Stay at home during the strike."

"It's easy for you to say so. But what about us?"

"We must learn to take risks."

"Yes, but I have a wife and kids!"

"There are wives and kids all over South Africa."

"But this looks like every man for himself. I must look after my own children."

"I wonder if your children will agree with you one day."

"My wife's all right. Mary understands. I can keep the kids from school for the strike. But Joe and I must work."

"And if you turn up and find all your colleagues stayed at home?"

"Then I come back."

"But you would have gone."

"Look, it's too big a sacrifice to expect from a family man."

"There are plenty of family men all over South Africa who are prepared to sacrifice."

"That might very well be, but the fact remains that if I don't report for work they might kick me out."

"So?"

"So where does a colored man find another job?"

"Where did you find the one you have now?"

"Will you politicians get me another?"

"Don't be silly."

"My kids will starve."

"So that their kids might eat one day."

"I'm not thinking of one day. I'm thinking of my children. Not in ten years' time or next year, but next month."

"I'm thinking of ten years' time."

"All very well for you to speak so, but I must consider my position."

"Think it over, but think fast. There isn't much time."

"I don't think there's anything to think over."

"Well, try at any rate."

Long Street was crowded with office workers, last-minute shoppers, women with babies, tramps, newspaper vendors, slick urban types, won't-works, bums. Boston and Lennie made their way toward the central area, edging and dodging between people. The noon gun boomed from Signal Hill. Boston adjusted his wrist watch.

"Must get to Castle Stationers before twelve-thirty," Lennie said.

"Why on earth?"

"I want to buy some drawing paper."

"Can't it wait?"

"No. I have to paint over the weekend."

"Hell. Must you go now?"

"It won't take a minute."

"We must get these pamphlets to Alec by one-thirty."

"We'll make it. There are plenty of buses."

"They're usually crowded at peak hour."

"We'll manage."

They weaved their way through the crowd. Boston stopped to buy a *Times*.

"What does it say?"

"The country's jittery. The whole damn South Africa's jittery."

"Strike fever?"

"What a way to welcome their new Republic." Boston accelerated his pace.

"You helping to distribute leaflets tonight?"

"No."

"Why the hell not?" Boston turned on him.

"I'm a painter, not a pseudo-politician."

"We're all in on this."

"Are? I've not been invited."

"That's not funny at all."

"Didn't intend it as such."

"Must you go through life as a cynic?"

"If you prefer it that way."

"Oh go to hell"

Boston always felt annoyed at Lennie when the conversation reached that stage. It had happened often before. He knew it was useless to continue in the same strain. He would start arguing, and the more excited he became, the more cynically Lennie would react. Finally it would sink to the level of personalities. He walked on moodily, refusing to continue the conversation.

"Cigarette?" Lennie asked.

"Peace offering?"

"Come off it."

"No, thanks."

"Oh, well. Artists of the world unite."

"Your world is so small."

"I love it."

"Comfortable, isn't it!" Boston sneered.

"Very. But it doesn't cramp my style."

"But then your style is extremely limited, isn't it?"

"Terribly so. Confined to posterity."

"What price arrogance!"

They continued their silent walk. Long Street was becoming less crowded. Bus queues stretched along the pavement.

"So?" Boston began, "meaning to paint masterpieces over the weekend?"

"One can but try."

"Except that one may succeed."

"That would be a pity. How is your novel getting on? Your answer to Dreiser? The Great South African Tragedy?"

"No time for writing these days. Too busy helping to organize a strike."

"How noble!"

"Yes, it's terribly hard work not being selfish."

"Behold I take upon my shoulders all the burdens of South Africa."

"Drop dead!"

"You started it."

"Did I?"

They continued without saying a word till they reached Castle Stationers.

"I'll wait outside," Boston said.

"All right."

"Now don't stay a helluva time."

Boston leaned against a lamp post and lit a cigarette. The newspaper was full of strike news. He scanned the headlines. HUGE GAS EXPLOSION AT COALBROOK. HIGH HEELS PREVENT CITY MAYOR'S HIKE. THOUSANDS ARRESTED IN MASS POLICE RAIDS. They're jittery, he thought, damn jittery. He hoped that Lennie wouldn't be long. There was Alec to meet at one-thirty.

Cape Town is ready to cope with strike. Every hope Republic will have peaceful birth. We, the people, are granite. Durban coloreds on the march. Transvaal coloreds up in arms.

Two men, one a young University student, dropping leaflets in letter boxes. Eleven-thirty P.M. in District Six.

"You take the next block. Be careful."

"Right. How many pamphlets are left?"

"Quite a few still in the car."

"I'll take the first ten houses. No dogs, I hope."

"Take my torch, but don't use it unless it's really necessary."

"This is sure risky."

"I know. Have a cigarette before you go."

"Thanks."

"First time you do it?"

"Yes."

"You'll learn."

"I suppose so."

"We still have six blocks to do."

"What's 'e time now?"

"Twenty-five to twelve."

"Looks like a police van!"

"Don't move. Keep still. No, it's okay."

"Oh, well. We breathe again."

"We must be careful. They're picking up too many of us."

"I hear they picked up Bill and Marjory last night."

"Yes, but Marjory's out. Bill's still in."

"Believe they went to a house and the owner phoned the police."

"Bloody swine!"

"In either case, it's better not to knock. Just slip the leaflet under the door or in the letter box."

"Then run."

"Not really, unless it's necessary."

"Okay. I'll tackle this row."

"Meet you at the car. I'll take the next block."

"All in order."

"See you later."

Boston finished his cigarette and stubbed it out impatiently against the lamp post. Damn, it was time Lennie came. He tried to do the crossword, 12 across. Discovered —a stout domestic penny. He gave it up. He glanced at his watch. Twelve-twenty and get to Alec by one-thirty. There was no use standing around. He might as well find Lennie inside and shake him up. He spotted him patiently standing at the crowded stationery counter while whites were being served first. His face was, as usual, impassive. Like an African Dan mask. One never knew what Lennie thought or felt unless he spoke. Boston tried to catch his eye, but Lennie stared stolidly ahead of him. Oh, well. Boston walked over to the bookshelves. His eyes ran over the titles. *Plays Pleasant, Pursuit of Love, The Floating Chinaman.* He removed the last-named from the shelf. What a giddy title. This is a book one must not read. Emphatically not. He replaced it.

Somehow he had a strong feeling that he was being watched. He looked around self-consciously. The shop was crowded, and no one looked as if they had time to pay any attention to him. There were so many books one must not read. Sex. Detection. Space fiction. Somehow he could not shake off the feeling of being watched. But then he always felt self-conscious about his presence in a crowd. Lennie still waiting to be served, and Alec to meet at one-thirty.

He removed *Modern American Short Stories* from the shelf. Hemingway, Katherine Porter, Erskine Caldwell. He glanced at the introduction. The Americans have a genius for the short story . . .

"May I help you?"

He looked up at the rather down-at-heel shop assistant in the pink smock.

"May I help you?"

"No, thanks. It's quite all right," he said, somewhat confused, "I'm waiting for someone. Just waiting." He half smiled at her.

"Are you sure?"

He detected a slight suspicion in her voice.

"Yes, quite sure. Why?"

"I only asked. Sorry." She turned around and walked away hurriedly.

Boston didn't like it. He wished to God Lennie would get done. Should he have come in? Should he have waited outside? Why the hell should he? He walked over to the stationery counter. One can't even look at books in a shop without attracting attention. He wished Lennie would finish so that they could get the hell out of the place. Meet Alec at one-thirty. It was now twelve-thirty. Christ, was it a crime for a colored man to read books in South Africa? Couldn't one even remove books from a shelf?

"Excuse me!"

Was every nonwhite a potential thief, pimp, liar?

"Excuse me!"

The manager stared down at him. Weak blue eyes peering through strong lenses, in contrast to his huge size. The assistant fidgeted at his side.

"Yes?"

"Miss Smart claims she saw you putting a book into your satchel." The assistant nodded agreement.

"Of all the bloody cheek!"

"Please control your language. Do you mind?"

"Mind what?"

"Opening your satchel."

"Yes, I do mind. I mind very much!"

"May I ask what you have in there?"

"*Encyclopaedia Britannica* and Van Riebeeck's *Journals.*"

"I'm not asking for your sarcasm."

"And I'm not asking for your cheek!"

"Will you please open your satchel?"

"I'm waiting for a friend!"

"That's not my business."

"Neither are the contents of my satchel!"

"Very well. If you insist on being difficult I shall have to call the police."

Boston felt strong resentment, humiliation. Had he

been a white man they would have taken him to the
privacy of the manager's office. A crowd collected. Must
he be subjected to all this? They could call the whole
bloody police force. He would not open his satchel.

"What's up?" Lennie inquired anxiously as he came
over.

"I'm accused of stealing books."

"Hell! So?"

"So they've gone to fetch the cops."

"That's bad!"

"What are we going to do?"

"We stay right here!"

"That could be nasty!"

"Well, I'm not a bloody thief!"

The crowd increased in size. The manager bustled his
way through, leading a police sergeant and an ordinary
constable.

"What's your name?" the sergeant demanded.

"Cloete. Boston Cloete."

"Age?"

"Twenty-seven years."

"Address?"

"Is that necessary?"

"Address?"

"Eight Church Street, Crawford."

"Where do you work?"

"I'm a writer."

"A what?"

"A writer!"

The crowd giggled. The sergeant noted down the details in his book.

"Well, then. Open your bag!"

Boston reluctantly started undoing the straps. The constable grabbed it from him and removed the brown paper parcel. He handed it to the sergeant.

"What's in here?"

"The Communist Manifesto, which I wrapped up before I stole it from the children's section."

The Sergeant glared at him, then commenced undoing the string. He removed a pamphlet and read it slowly. His eyes hardened.

"Oh, I see," he said, "I'll give you Communist Manifesto! Come along with me!"

AZIKWELWA

by James Matthews

He did not have to walk. He looked over his shoulder at the hundreds coming along behind him, all walking, and in front of him hundreds more, walking. It was the fifth day of their long walk to Johannesburg and it was his first. He was one of the few coloreds who walked along with the mass of Africans. They were old and young, big and small, foot-firm and limping; mothers and sons, fathers and daughters, grandparents and school-children; some dressed in neat clothes with horn-rimmed glasses and attaché cases, and many more in torn overalls and shoes with soles paper-thin, feeling each stone they trod on. They were all walking the long walk to Johannesburg.

Nights before the boycott was due, the location's fast-

35

beating heart increased its pace. Wherever a man raised his voice, a group formed around him, and as the hours passed, there were many such groups, until the location throbbed one great meeting place. There were the wild ones whose eyes saw only violence and their cry was, "Burn the buses!" Then there were those few who whispered, "Accept the terms." But there were also the many who defiantly said, "Azikwelwa! We will not ride!"

When they started their walk the sky was still dark under the pulsating stars. He watched them from the inside of his room, and after a time went back to the warmth of his blankets. Later he had a bus to himself on the ride to the station. There were angry voices when he boarded the bus, but those who shouted loudest were restrained by others with rosettes pinned to their breasts. Then, when the bus passed the long firm line of walkers, he heard their cry again. His return from work found them homeward bound, a song traveling their length. A stone hit the side of the bus and he peered through the rear window. Four men were shaking a youth by the shoulders, and then they all disappeared from view as the bus turned a bend in the road.

As if by a prearranged plan, the location's streets swarmed with people who embraced each other and sang at the top of their voices. In the backyards of the shebeen queens, skokiaan flowed freely for those who had the money to pay for it. And even those who came with empty pockets were given something for their throats. As they faced one another they cried, "Azikwelwa! My brother."

Four days he watched them walk the long walk and four nights he saw them dance and drink their tiredness away, and the spirit of their pride filled him. Their word was as good as that of the white man. They said they would walk the many miles before paying the extra penny the bus company demanded. There were many whites who scoffed at their determination, and there was their answer, in the line of empty buses. On the fifth morning, when the first wave of walkers had passed his door, he joined them. From side streets poured rushes of walkers, and the mass of people flowed through the gates of the location.

On his left walked an old man who used a stick to help him along, and in front of him waddled a fat woman with a bundle of washing balanced on her head. He looked around him. There were many such women, and some had babies strapped to their backs, the heads of the babies jogging with the motion of their mothers' hips.

It was still early and the first mile was not done and they were in a holiday mood. Bicycles carried two passengers. The location's ancient cars, which always threatened to fall apart, were loaded to capacity and wheezed their way forward. One man, his boots tied around his neck, joked with his friend and said that it made for easier walking. All joined in the laughter. There were walking the long walk and they were proud.

The miles passed and the road was long and there was less laughter, but still they walked. The old, the sick, the weak dropped behind. The front of the column was wide, but behind it tapered off to a thin line of stragglers.

Then suddenly there were the police and the cars standings in rows and the people inside pulled out and forced to the side of the road. And the owners protested that the cars were not used as taxis, but they were still charged with overloading. The harsh demands for passes, and the fearful swelling as they waited for the vans to take them away. Then the next block of police waiting with outstretched hands and ready batons for those who had not the slips of paper which gave them the right to move. There were many who slipped down side streets to escape the police, for the police wanted them to ride and not walk, so that there should be no strength of will and so that they should be without a voice.

"Pass! Where is it?" he was asked. The owner of the voice was not bothering to look at him, and only when he made no reply, turned his eyes.

"I don't carry a pass," he replied.

"Then what are you doing here?"

"I am walking!"

"Are you a Kaffir or are you a Communist?"

"I am walking!"

38

He walked past the policeman, who had already grasped another victim by the shirt front, demanding his pass.

A large car pulled to a halt in front of him, behind the wheel a young white woman. She opened the doors on each side and cried aloud, "Come on. Women and old people." No one moved. Then a woman with a child on her back and a suitcase in one hand shyly approached the car and got into the back. Others followed, but the old man shook his head, saying that he was not too old to finish the long walk. More cars stopped and their drivers were white and they took those who wanted to ride.

A car stopped and the driver asked the young policeman by whose orders he was stopping the car and demanding the removal of the passengers. He stood undecided and the car pulled away. He rushed to the nearest man and screamed, "You Kaffirs think you're smart!"

Messages were relayed from those arrested to those free. Messages to tell a father a son was arrested, to assure an employer that an employee would come back to his job, to tell the children not to worry and to help each other.

And those who walked were still many and their hearts were heavy, but they walked, and soon the long walk was at an end, for below them was the city. On their entry into the city, the people of the city looked at them with disbelief, and their shoulders straightened and their heads lifted and they smiled. They had done the long walk one more day.

It was late when he entered the chemist shop where he worked as a delivery messenger.

"Jonathan. Why are you late?"

"I walked."

"All the way?" The white man in the white coat looked at him with surprise.

"All the way."

"But why? You're not one of them."

He could not tell the white man of the feeling inside him, that when he was with them he knew it was good.

He joined them on the square at midday. They sat with mugs of coffee and still-hot fat cakes bought from the portable coffee stalls of the vendors. Some sat around draught boards, using bottle tops as counters, but most were clustered around those with newspapers. There were pictures on the front page showing the many walkers, and the reports stated that the boycott would soon be over and that the leaders of the boycott had come to an agreement. There were angry murmurs amongst them, and some said aloud that they did not believe it. One man said what they all had on their minds. "Why is it that we were not approached? Are we not the people who walk? Does the bus company think because it has spoken to a few men, we, like sheep, will now meekly ride instead of walk?"

The last question was directed at one who wore the colors of the boycott organization on his breast at night in the location.

He was a short, wiry man and his eyes blinked behind the thick-lensed glasses he wore. He took them off, wiped the lenses nervously with his handkerchief, and replaced the glasses on the bridge of his wide, flat nose. He cleared his throat before speaking and then, in a surprisingly loud voice, said, "Do not believe it, my brothers. It is not for our leaders to say we walk or ride before first asking the will of the people of the location. The men of the bus company must think our leaders are but children to be so easily swayed by their words. Pay no heed to what is written in the newspapers because it is the word of the white man."

His words reassured them, but there were the few, already tired of the long walk, who said it was a good thing. "The white man has seen that the black man is also a man of his word." Now they would ride.

Jonathan was filled with doubt. Always he was with those who suffered without protest. Always he was with those without voice. Always he was with those who had to bear the many pains. Always he was with those unwanted, and always they lost.

He had secretly thought that the boycott would only last the first day, then the people of the location with their tired limbs would once more ride the buses and their purpose would die. But when it entered the second day, the third day, and the day after that, his hopes mounted, hoping that this would be the one time they would prove themselves men. It had become a symbol to him. As long as they walked, his life would not be altogether meaningless. He would be able to say with pride that he too was one of those who had walked the long walk, when they proved to the bus company that they had a will of their own and were not to be silenced into obedience by words.

During all his deliveries Jonathan was depressed, and when he read the afternoon paper, his despair swamped him, and he felt cold in the afternoon sun. He felt betrayed. The paper stated that an agreement had been reached and that the following morning the buses would be filled. The boycott would be over.

To forget, he busied himself with his work and was relieved when given a stack of deliveries that would keep him occupied for the rest of the afternoon.

Work done, he joined the lines of walkers ascending the first incline out of the city. They were a silent lot, and when someone asked if it was to be the last day of the long walk, he was answered with shrugs of the shoulders and shaking of heads in bewilderment. The lines merged into one long column of heavy hearts and dragging feet. There were no jokes, no laughter. Only doubts and uncertainty, the ringing footsteps turned into drumbeats of defeat.

The walk was long and the road without end. The cars stopped, and they looked without interest at those who climbed inside. With apprehension they passed the first group of grinning policemen, and when they were not stopped, their betrayal seemed complete.

A youth raised his voice and said loudly: "Azikwelwa!" And he was cursed by some around him. But he would not be denied and he repeated it louder, his voice carrying farther: "Azikwelwa! My brothers and sisters!" Those who heard the youth's outburst turned their heads and stared at him, and they buzzed with curiosity.

"Has news been heard?" "Do we do the long walk tomorrow?" "What has happened?" They shouted but there was no answer. Then a voice cried, "We will hear tonight in the location," and it was taken up and passed along the ranks. And the stride of the walkers increased, and Jonathan's heart kept pace with their footsteps.

They passed further blocks of policemen, and there were no stoppings, and there was not the demand for passes. And the cars loaded with people passed unchallenged. And the miles slipped behind as they hurried to the location.

His supper ended, Jonathan walked with the others to the football field where the boycott organization held its meetings, and pushed himself to the front. The field filled, and when he turned his head the back of the field was blocked out by the bodies of the many people.

A speaker mounted an upended crate, his hands held aloft. It was the same man who had spoken on the square during the afternoon. His voice roared.

"The bus company has taken it on itself, after speaking to those who could never speak for us, to have it printed in the papers of the white man that the boycott is ended! Is done with! That we have, like little children, agreed to their talks and will board the buses tomorrow. But they are wrong. This is our answer. Azikwelwa! Azikwelwa! . . ." The rest of the speech was lost in the clamor pouring from the open throats, and when other speakers tried to speak they met with the same result. The people of the location needed no further speeches, and the crowd spilled apart.

Again the backyards of the shebeen queens were flooded and skokiaan was to be had for the asking.

Jonathan sat on a bench with his mug of skokiaan untouched, a bemused smile on his face. Opposite, a drinker was slumped against the wall and his wife looked boldly at Jonathan. Looking at her, and with the people swarming around him, Jonathan felt a surge of love sweeping through his body and he raised his mug to the woman.

"Azikwelwa! My sister," he said.

AWENDGESANG

by Alf Wannenburgh

OLD FRANS FEBRUARY stood on a flat rock at the summit of the pass and watched as his people assembled in the clearing before him.

Four miles behind them to the north lay the settlement at Elandskloof, which they had left at sunrise that very morning. Now they were encamped on the pass for the night, with the dark outline of the Sederberg Mountains rising above them to the east, and the Olifants River, running deep with the late winter rains, below them to the west. And somewhere in the lands to the south—in the hundred miles between themselves and the sea—somewhere, they hoped, there might be a new home, where they could again enjoy the things that had been taken from them.

Now they were coming down from the scattered, small fires on the slopes to the clearing, and as they assembled they sang:

"Gee my die oude tydings,
Gee my die oude tydings,
Gee my die oude tydings . . ."

A fire had been built in the center of the clearing, and the flames from the fast-burning brush shot high into the congealing darkness, tinting the varicolored headcloths of the women with shades of red and orange, giving inconstant light to the weather-scarred surfaces of the surrounding rocks and dust-laden bushes.

Old Frans February stood on a flat rock at the summit of the pass and watched them with paternal fondness. He had been born into the community long before most of them, and for the past thirty years he had been chairman of their small committee, the Elandskloof Vigilance Association. He knew intimately every one of the almost six hundred faces now grouped around the fire. Behind those collarless shirts and soiled waistcoats—remnants of long-forgotten suits—enclosed in those shapeless jackets, he knew every sorrow and every gladness. It was to him that they brought their troubles and disputes, and it was with him that they shared their every joy. And so it was now, as their leader, that he partook of the great communal sorrow that had come to them all.

46

When he raised his Bible and opened it the singing faded and ceased. And he read to them:

"O Heere! wie is als Gij onder de goden? Who is like unto thee, O Lord, among the gods? Who is like thee glorious in holiness, fearful in praises, doing wonders?"

And then the people murmured, "Amen."

And he paused and prayed silently: In the wilderness, Heavenly Father, are your children: the aged and infirm, the young and the sucklings. Behind them they have left their homes and their animals, all that they have ever had.

"Gij leiddet door Uwe weldadigheid dit volk, dat Gij verlest hebt. Thou in thy mercy hast led forth the people which thou hast redeemed: Thou hast guided them in thy strength unto thy holy habitation. Gij voert hen zachtkens door Uwe sterkte tot de liefelijke woning Uwer heiligheid."

And he remembered that in twelve hours they had traveled only four miles. Twelve hours without food, for the decision to leave had been sudden, and there had been no time to bake the bread for the journey. Before sunrise, the owner of the land on which the community had lived for a hundred years had come to the settlement and said that the years of argument had come to an end, and that they must be gone by nightfall. And so behind them they had left their homes and their animals.

And he was afraid for the future. For the hindrances that would be placed in their path, for the actions which would be taken against them. Now already it was said

that the authorities wished to divide and distribute them
among the farmers as laborers. Their desire to remain together found no favor with those who had the strength
to compel. So that now, all six hundred of them together,
they would have to wander through the countryside until
they found their new home.

"Fear and dread shall fall upon them; by the greatness
of thine arm they shall be still as a stone, till thy people
pass over, O Heere, till the people pass over, which thou
hast purchased."

But still there was reason for them to fear, for the
tragedies which had befallen those who went against the
will of the authorities were well known.

"Thou shalt bring them in, and plant them in the
mountain of thine inheritance, in the place, O Heere,
which thou hast made for thee to dwell in, in the
Sanctuary, O Heere, which thy hands have established."

And the people sang again:

> *"Gee my die oude tydings,*
> *Tell me the old old story,*
> *Tell me the old old story,*
> *Of Jesus and his love . . ."*

He raised both hands above him, and once more the
singing ceased.

"Brothers and sisters, we are gathered here tonight to
praise God, and to seek His guidance in the days that lie
ahead of us. Our homes have been taken away from us,

and we wander at His mercy in the wilderness. We must speak of these things, for if we have faith in His power to heal our suffering, it is through our speech then that he will reveal His plan to us."

And the first who spoke were those who had been members of the Vigilance Association for many years:

"All my life have I lived at Elandskloof," said one who was also on the committee of the Mothers' Union of the mission church. "My parents and their parents before them are buried there, as also the three children who came dead from my womb. Now I must leave untended the graves of those whom I loved, because this white farmer has bought the land we always thought was ours."

"And I," said another. "Thirty years ago I bought my house from the church. How was I then to know that they would sell the land I lived on? All the money that I have earned on other men's farms I have used to build sties for my pigs and hoks for my chickens, so that I would not be a burden to my children in my old age. Now there is nothing."

"And these people in the City," said yet another, "they tell us that we must go to the farms and that the farmers will give a place to sleep, to those who will work on their lands. But what of the crippled and blind among us who can no longer work? Where will they find a place to sleep?"

"What of the old and gray whom together we have been able to care for?"

"Yes, what of the old and gray?"

"What of the children in the schools?"

"Yes, what of the children in the schools?"

"And what of the children to come?"

"Yes, what of the children to come?"

And so the people spoke of the things that were heavy on their minds.

Frans February seated himself on the rock and listened as they spoke. One after the other they stood up and repeated what those before them had said, and often they spoke the same thing many times in the same words, but always telling of their own losses and hardships and those which they shared, always speaking of what had been done to them—never of what they would do. And he knew that it would be as always it was: that any decisions would be of his making. It was true that sometimes, when they were angry or desperate, there would be a spontaneous, undiscussed decision to act, as had been the case when they had left Elandskloof that morning. But when they were asked to consider any other thing or what they should do, then it was as if their responsibility had suddenly come to an end the moment it had been decided that he would lead them. It was always for him to decide. They left it to him. They always did.

And he knew that it would be as always it was.

Then it was that Dirk Jaftha came forward to speak. He was the youngest member of the Vigilance Committee, and had been in the Cape Corps and had fought in

Egypt and Italy during the war. And the people were silent at first, because they knew he had seen far more of the world than they had.

"Friends," he said, "all we ask is a place where we can live together and work in happiness."

And the people nodded their heads, because they felt with what he said.

"It is not we alone who search. All over this country there are people, like ourselves, who are searching for the same thing."

Then there was a low rumble of disapproval from the old people, for what he said sounded like politics. But Frans February raised his hand and said: "Let him speak." And they were still.

"They are like us because they also do not know where they will find such a place. But can any of us find it on our own!"

Once more the old people shook their heads, and this time they called on him to stop speaking of things which concerned other people, but which did not concern them. And once more Frans February said that they should allow Dirk Jaftha to speak.

"There is no Promised Land for us alone, and we cannot find it alone. Things are changing. But if we stand together and show these others that we shall not be moved from our plan, then there must be a day when they will join us. And together with them we shall make this the Promised Land."

Now the murmurings of the old people were angry, and whereas, before, they had respected him because of what he had seen of the world, they now said: "To think that he was born among us. There is his mother, who is eighty years old—almost as old as Frans February. You can see that he has been away from his people. You can see what it has done to him. He can no longer speak like us. He is no longer one of us."

But Frans February did not listen to the murmurings of the old people, for all the while that Dirk Jaftha had spoken, he had watched the faces of the younger people; and he had noticed the new light of excitement that had come to their eyes and the secret smiles of agreement that had been on their lips while Dirk Jaftha spoke. And he was uncertain.

While the old people were still murmuring, Manie Damens came to the front of the assembly. He did not belong to the community by birth, but had come to it as a teacher in the mission school twenty-five years before, in the days when the settlement at Elandskloof was still controlled by the church. When it had withdrawn its support from the school, he had remained to teach the children, depending on the community to supply him with food, clothing and shelter. And when the white farmer had locked the door of the school, he had continued to teach them in the fields.

Because he wished to speak, the people were silent. After all, he was a teacher, a man of education.

"People of Elandskloof," he said. "We have heard the words of Dirk Jaftha. But we know that the things he says are the things they say in the City. We are not people of the City. We are people of the country."

And the people nodded their heads, because they believed that what he said was true.

"We are people of the country who know that it is best that we follow the guidance of the older and wiser among us."

Then the people clapped their hands and called out their approval.

"And who is older and wiser, who has served us better as chairman of the Elandskloof Vigilance Committee—who but Meneer Frans February?"

The agreement of the people was loud, and they said to each other: "He was not born among us. And you can see that there is not one of his family here. But you can also see that he has *lived* with us. He speaks as we do. He is one of us."

And again Frans February watched the faces of the younger people; and he saw that there was no light of excitement in their eyes, no smile of agreement on their lips, and that it was not they who raised their voices in approval.

He knew that it would be as always it was.

When the old people left the clearing and returned to their individual fires on the slopes, Frans February climbed a short way up above the pass and stood high

over the encamped community, his back resting against
the raw surface of the night-darkened rock. The overcast
sky was lighted from behind the clouds by a full moon,
which rested like an incandescent cupola on the rim of
the horizon. In the half light, from where he stood, he had
an unobscured view, for a few hundred yards, of the
road as it wound its corrugated, pothole-pitted descent
to the foot of the pass. And six miles away, in the valley,
he could see the patch of scattered lights that vaguely
defined the ragged limits of the first town through which
they would have to pass.

Now that he was on his own, away from his people,
he felt tired and weak, and the weight of his responsibility lay heavily on him. He placed his hands behind
him and pressed his palms against the chill, unyielding
surface of the rock. And the uncertainty he had first felt
beside the fire in the clearing returned in a great strength-
sapping wave, and he doubted his ability to lead his
people. He was afraid. For then he knew that there was a
way in which a man thinks with his lips when he was
with those whom he must lead, and a way in which he
thinks in his heart when he is alone.

Down below him, in the clearing, the younger people
had gathered around the fire, and again they were
singing:

> "Gee my die oude tydings,
> Tell me the old old story,
> Tell me the old old story,
> Of Jesus and his love . . ."

As he listened to the words of the old hymn, it was as if they were singing:

"Gee my die oude tyde,
Gee my die oude tyde . . ."

and asking for the return of the old days of their happiness, for the word "tydings" was distorted by the acoustics of the rocks to sound like "tyde," which means "times." And at first he smiled, because the distortion was appropriate. And then he was sad, for he knew that they would never again enjoy the old times. No, the old times had passed; but life would go on—they would go on—and there would be new and unfamiliar times into which he would have to lead them. And, maybe, a Promised Land.

And as he thought of the Promised Land, of which he knew nothing, the words of Isaiah returned to him—a passage which was among his favorites—and softly, to himself, he repeated them:

"They shall build houses, and inhabit them; and they shall plant vineyards, and eat the fruit of them . . . for as the days of a tree are the days of my people, and mine elect shall long enjoy the work of their hands."

He drew fresh strength from the vision of the future contained in the words he repeated, and once more he believed in his own ability to lead the people. But then he remembered the faces of the younger ones beside the fire; how they had been excited by the words of Dirk Jaftha, and how the flame of their excitement had been extinguished by the reply of Manie Damens. And then he knew that it was only the old ones who still had faith in him—only they who believed that there was a Promised Land to which he could lead them. Again he felt the tiredness of age and was afraid of the temptations which would prey upon his weakness, and lead him into accepting conditions which would not have tempted a younger man. And he wondered at the simplicity of a manner of living which depended on one as weak as himself.

Below him the people continued to sing:

> *"Gee my die oude tyde,*
> *Gee my die oude tydings,*
> *Tell me the old old story,*
> *Of Jesus and his love . . ."*

Grouped as they were, in shades of red and copper around the fire, the younger people reminded him of the petals of a varkblom in bud—closed together in protection of the seeds, which promised new beauties and joys. It was all that the older generations could give them, this spirit of community.

Yes, times were changing and sweeping everything before them, bringing fresh ideas and new ways of doing things. And still he was left with the responsibility of leadership, and would be called upon to do things his religion would not allow. But then, all was being pushed aside—the old way of life, the old religion, and even the old ways of protesting. Everything would change, and then he too would be pushed aside. Perhaps Dirk Jaftha was right, for there would be new leaders, and the youth would go out and distribute the seed of the varkblom. And yes, there would be a Promised Land.

". . . want de dagen Mijns volks zullen zijn als de dagen eens booms. For the days of a tree are the days of my people, and mine elect shall long enjoy the work of their hands. Zullen het werk hunner handen verslijten."

And there would still be youth.

Then he looked again over the land to the south. The clouds had thickened and become so heavy that they excluded the light of the moon. And he saw that the road along which he would have to lead the people was now in darkness.

OUT OF
THE DARKNESS
by Alex La Guma

THE SMELL of unwashed bodies and sweaty blankets
was sharp, and the heat in the cell hung as thick as cotton
wool.

The man on the rope mat beside me turned, grunted,
and flung a long arm across my face.

"How do you do?" he said, waking up and giggling.

"Very well," I replied soothingly, for he was a little
mad.

In the dark the other bodies turned, cursed, and tried
to settle back into perspiring sleep.

"Did Joey bring the eggs?"

I could make out the dim shapeless bulge of his body
curled up on the mat. He had entered the seventh year

of his ten-year sentence for culpable homicide, and being shut up so long had unhinged him somewhat. He was neither staring mad nor violent. His insanity was of a gentle quality that came in spells. It was then that he would talk. Otherwise he was clamped up tight and retired, like a snail withdrawn into its shell. He was friendly enough, but it was the friendliness of a man on the other side of a peephole.

To the rest of the inmates he was known as Ou Kakkelak, Old Cockroach, and was either the butt of their depraved humor or was completely ignored. He took everything with a gentle smile. From parts of his conversations during his spells I gained the impression that he was an educated man and might have been a schoolmaster before he had committed his crime.

"Cora," he went on in the dark. "You know, I like that part where Juliet dies over Romeo's body."

From somewhere beyond the high barred window came the steady crunch of boots as a guard passed in the night.

"Is the heat troubling you?" I asked, as kindly as I could make it. "It's damn hot, isn't it?" He did not reply. I decided to do a little probing. "You speak of Cora now and then. Who is she?" But he turned on his side and was asleep again.

In the morning there was the usual shouting and clanging of doors. Blankets were folded; the long line of convicts streamed down to the yards. The guards stood by, lashing out with leather belts.

"Spring bliksems! Come on, you black bastards!"

We squatted, packed into the cement yard, and break-fasted on mealie meal and black, bitter coffee. Old Cock-roach sat near me, smiling his gentle, vacant smile and wolfing his food.

I saw him again when we were locked up after supper. He sank down in his place beside me. Around us secret cigarettes were emerging, the primitive flint and steel contraptions were struck, and smoke drifted up from be-hind cupped fingers. Figures in washed-out red shirts and canvas shorts packed the floor of the cell.

"Here we are," Old Cockroach said and giggled at me. "The wreckage which mankind, on its onward march, left behind."

"Well," I answered, smiling at him. "Perhaps it's better to say that we are the results of mankind's imperfections."

"Perhaps. Perhaps. I wonder where Joey is tonight." He sat with his knees drawn up and his long arms clasped about his shins, gazing vacantly about at the faces around him. "Ah, there he is now."

I looked and said, "That's Smiley Abrams. Remember? That's not Joey. That's Smiley Abrams."

"Oh, *ja*. He's here for murder. I believe he's killed three people in his lifetime. They got him for the last one. An ape-man roaming a jungle. Here he is king. In a cave the cave man is king."

He fell silent again. Around us conversation took the form of a low muttering that formed a ragged buzzing.

61

I sat with my back against the concrete wall and looked at Old Cockroach. He was tall and thin and bony, folded up now like a carpenter's ruler. His skin was as dark as burnt leather, and he had slightly negroid features and kinky hair going gray, close to his skull, like a tight-fitting cap.

"This place is like an oven," I said, trying to build up another conversation.

"Cora," he rambled. "I think . . ."

"She'll turn up on visiting day," I told him, although I knew she would not, whoever she was, because nobody had ever visited him for as long as I had been in. I began to wish I could learn more about him.

From outside came the scrape and thump of boots on the stone staircase. Steel gratings clanged like boilers being opened and closed. Silence fell in the stone casern with the finality of sound on a radio being switched off. Cigarettes were killed and carefully concealed, and each man retreated quickly within himself and looked dumb.

Through the peephole in the heavy, studded door a voice trumpeted angrily. "Hou julle bekke! Shut your filthy mouths, you bastards . . ."

The silence remained inside, a cautious, discreet silence that hung like a veil while the gratings clanged and the footsteps receded. When they had faded completely, the veil was lifted slowly and carefully as the broken murmurs came out of hiding.

Smiley Abrams climbed to his feet, kicked a pathway

through the sprawling humanity around him, and plodded deliberately toward the door. His great shoulders hunched under the torn red shirt. He hawked and spat straight onto the door and wiped his mouth on the back of his hand. Then he turned and stalked back along the pathway to his place.

"Just a warning." Old Cockroach smiled. "No, not meant for those 'corpies.' He can't afford to be hardcase with them. That was really meant for us all. The ape must make it known that he is still king of the jungle, even if the elephant is bigger than he is."

The sun faded beyond the barred windows like lights being dimmed in a theater. It had become hot again in the casern, and from the bucket latrine came the sharp, acid smell of ammonia. Old Cockroach lay back on his mat and pulled the thin blanket up to his waist. He did not seem to feel the heat, but just lay there, calmly gazing at the dim bulb in the whitewashed stone ceiling. It was as if he had drawn an invisible armor around himself.

"Have you any family, old man?" I asked, gently attacking the armor.

"Huh?" He looked blank and then smiled softly at me.

"A man's got to have somebody. People." But the armor was tightly strapped and riveted.

The next night started much the same. The heat was overpowering, and the stench of bodies increased quickly. Men fought and clawed around the water buckets, snarl-

ing like jackals around their carrion. The cave man,
Smiley Abrams, hurled men from the center of the tur-
moil, growling and snapping at his cringing subjects.
A man rose to challenge him. A great, clubbed fist drew
back and then struck with the sound of a pick handle
against a pumpkin. The rebel went down like a stricken
ox and lay still, to be trampled by the others.

"A slave has revolted," Old Cockroach observed in a
voice as gentle as the fall of dust. "Do you know that
the whole of mankind's history consists of a series of
revolutions?"

"You're an educated man, Old Cockroach," I said.
"You don't belong here. How did you come to kill anybody? If you don't mind me asking."

"I used to be a schoolmaster," he replied, confirming
my old suspicion. Then his mind wandered again, and he
murmured, "I hope Joey brings that book he borrowed
last week. *Treasure Island*. Have you ever read *Treasure
Island?*"

"Yes. Long ago, when I was a pikkie."

The brawl around the water buckets had subsided, since
they both had been emptied. There would be no water for
the rest of the night. Men sat around, hunched stark
naked under the light, exploring their clothes and
blankets for lice. The cracking of vermin between thumb-
nails sounded like snapping twigs. My own body was
slippery with sweat.

It was no better with the light turned off. The cloying heat and the stench of the latrine seemed to take advantage of the darkness. Old Cockroach had settled down on his blankets and I could hear him scratching himself. I was doing the same, and sleep became impossible. From all around us grunts, curses, and tiny cries came like suppressed voices out of hell.

". . . Cora," Old Cockroach's voice came out of the dark, quiet as the trickle of sweat. "Cora."

"Take it easy, old man," I murmured.

"Oh, you're not Cora . . ."

"Nay, man. Sorry, though."

Silence.

I decided to probe a little more. "By the way, who is Cora?"

Silence. Then he said, "Hullo, Joey. I'm glad you've come. I'll tell you a story. Would you like to listen to a story?"

"Okay. That would be fine."

"All right, then. It was a long time ago. A very long time ago, I think. I was in love with her. You don't think this is going to be a silly story, do you?"

"Certainly not."

"I was a teacher at a junior school and was doing a varsity course in my spare time. And I was in love with Cora. She was beautiful. Really beautiful. Her skin was soft and smooth and the color of rich cream. She was almost white, you see. I was in love with her. We had grown up together in Dublin Street in Woodstock, and

I think I must have been in love with her as long as I can remember.

"I became a schoolmaster. We were going to be married, and I worked hard because I wanted her to have everything that would make her happy once we were married."

He was silent again while the sounds of sleep went on around us. When he went on his voice had taken on a dullness. "Then she began to find that she could pass for white. She could pass as white, and I was black. She began to go out to white places, bioscopes, cafés. Places where I couldn't take her. She met white people who thought she was really white, and they invited her out to their homes. She went to parties and dances. She drifted away from me, but I kept on loving her.

"I talked to her, pleaded with her. But she wouldn't take any notice of what I said. I became angry. I wept. I raved. Can you imagine how much I loved her? I groveled. I was prepared to lose my entire self-respect just to keep her. But it wasn't of any use. She said I was selfish and trying to deny her the good things of life. The good things of life. I would have given her anything I *could*. And she said I was denying her the good things of life.

"In the end she turned on me. She told me to go to hell. She slapped my face and called me a black nigger. A black nigger."

"Then you lost your head and killed her," I said quietly. "That's why you're here now."

66

"Oh, no," Old Cockroach answered. "I could never have done that to Cora. I did lose my head, but it was Joey whom I killed. He said I was a damn fool for going off over a damn play-white bitch. So I hit him, and he cracked his skull on something. Ah, here's Joey now. Hullo, Joey. I hope you've brought my book . . ."

The Dispossessed

*Our inequality
materializes our upper classes,
vulgarizes our middle classes,
brutalizes our lower classes.*
—MATTHEW ARNOLD

RESURRECTION

by Richard Rive

THE PEOPLE SANG. And one by one the voices
joined in and the volume rose. Tremulously at first,
thin and tenuous, and then swelling till it filled the tiny
dining room, pulsated into the two bedrooms, stacked
high with hats and overcoats, and spent itself in the
kitchen where fussy housewives, dressed in black, were
making wreaths.

> *"Jesu lover of my soul,*
> *Let me to Thy bo-som fly . . ."*

A blubbery woman in the corner nearest the cheap,
highly polished chest of drawers wept hysterically. Above
her head hung a cheap reproduction of a Karroo scene.
A dazzling white-gabled farmhouse baking in the hot

African sun, in the distance kopjes shimmering against a hazy blue sky. Her bosom heaved and her lips quivered as she refused to be placated. Her tears proved infectious and handkerchiefs were convulsively sought.

> *"Hide me, O my Saviour, hide,*
> *Till the storm of life is past;*
> *Safe into the haven guide . . ."*

sang a small boy in a freshly laundered Eton collar who shared a stiff Ancient and Modern Hymnbook with his mother. His voice was wiry and weak and completely dominated by the strong soprano next to him. All the people joined in and sang. Except Mavis. Only Mavis sat silent, glossy-eyed, staring down at her rough though delicately shaped brown hands. Her eyes hot and red, but tearless, with a slightly contemptuous sneer around the closed, cruel mouth. Only Mavis sat silent. Staring at her hands and noticing that the left thumbnail was scarred and broken. She refused to raise her eyes, refused to look at the coffin, at the hymnbook open and neglected on her lap. Her mouth was tightly shut, as if determined not to open, not to say a word. Tensely she sat and stared at her broken fingernail. The room did not exist. The fat woman blubbered unnoticed. The people sang but Mavis heard nothing.

> *"Other refuge have I none,*
> *Hangs my helpless soul on Thee . . ."*

they began the second verse. The fat woman had sufficiently recovered to attempt to add a tremulous contralto. The boy in the Eton collar laboriously followed the line with his finger. Mavis vaguely recognized Rosie as she fussily hurried in with a tray of fresh flowers, passed a brief word with an overdressed woman nearest the door, and busily hurried out again. Mavis sensed things happening but saw without seeing and felt without feeling. Nothing registered, but she could feel the Old Woman's presence, could feel the room becoming her dead mother, becoming full of Ma, crowded with Ma, swirling with Ma. Ma of the gnarled hands and frightened eyes. Those eyes that had asked questioningly, "Mavis, why do they treat me so? Please Mavis, why do they treat me so?"

And Mavis had known the answer and had felt the anger well up inside her, till her mouth felt hot and raw. And she had spat out at the Old Woman, "Because you're colored! You're colored, Ma, but you gave birth to white children. It's your fault, Ma, all your fault. . . . You gave birth to white children. White children, Ma. White Children!"

Mavis felt dimly aware that the room was overcrowded, overbearingly overcrowded. Hot, stuffy, crammed, overflowing. And, of course, Ma. Squeezed in. Occupying a tiny place in the center. Right in the center. Pride of place in a coffin of pinewood that bore the economical legend:

Maria Loupser
1889-1961
R.I.P.

Rest in peace. With people crowding around and sharing seats and filling the doorway. And Ma had been that Maria Loupser who must now rest in peace. Maria Loupser. Maria Wilhelmina Loupser. Mavis looked up quickly to see if the plaque was really there, then automatically shifted her gaze to her broken nail. No one noticed her self-absorption, and the singing continued uninterruptedly.

> *"Other refuge have I none,*
> *Hangs my helpless soul on Thee . . ."*

Flowers. Hot, oppressive smell of flowers. Flowers, death, and the people singing. A florid red-faced man in the doorway singing so that his veins stood out purple against the temples. People bustling in and out. Fussily. Coming to have a look at Ma. A last look at Ma. To put a flower in the coffin for Ma. Then opening hymnbooks and singing a dirge for Ma. Poor deceived Ma of the tragic eyes and twisted hands who had given birth to white children, and Mavis. Now they raised their voices and sang for Ma.

> *"Leave, ah, leave me not alone,*
> *Still support and comfort me! . . ."*

74

And it had been only a month earlier when Mavis had looked into those bewildered eyes.

"Mavis, why do they treat me so?"

And Mavis had become angry so that her saliva had turned hot in her mouth.

"Please Mavis, why do they treat me so?"

And then she had driven the words into the Old Woman with a skewer.

"Because you are old and black, and your children want you out of the way."

And yet what Mavis had wanted to add was, "They want me out of the way too, Ma, because you made me black like you. I am also your child, Ma. I belong to you. They want me also to stay in the kitchen and use the back door. We must not be seen, Ma, their friends must not see us. We embarrass them, Ma, so they hate us. They hate us because we're black. You and I, Ma."

But she had not said so, and had only stared cruelly into the eyes of the Old Woman. Eyes that did not understand. Eyes already dying. And she had continued to torture the Old Woman.

"You're no longer useful, Ma. You're a nuisance, a bloody nuisance, a bloody black nuisance. You might come out of your kitchen and shock the white scum they bring here. You're a bloody nuisance, Ma!"

But still the Old Woman could not understand, and looked helplessly at Mavis.

"But I don't want to go in the dining room. It's true, Mavis, I don't want to go in the dining room."

And as she spoke tears flooded her eyes and she whimpered like a child who had lost a toy.

"It's my dining room, Mavis, it's true. It's my dining room."

And Mavis had felt such a dark and hideous pleasure overwhelming her that she had screamed hysterically at the Old Woman.

"You're black and your bloody children's white. Jim and Rosie and Sonny are white, white, white! And you made me. You made me black!"

Then Mavis had broken down exhausted at her self-revealing and had cried like a baby.

"Ma, why did you make me black?"

And then only had a vague understanding strayed into those milky eyes, and Ma had taken her youngest into her arms and rocked and soothed her. And crooned to her in a cracked, broken voice the songs she had sung years before she had come to Cape Town.

"Slaap my kindjie slaap sag,
Onder engele vannag. . . ."

And the voice of the Old Woman had become stronger and more perceptive as her dull eyes saw her childhood, and the stream running through Wolfgat, and the broken-down church, and the moon rising in the direction of Solitaire.

And Ma had understood and rocked Mavis in her arms like years before. And now Ma was back in the dining room as shadows crept across the wall.

"Abide with me! Fast falls the eventide. . . ."

Shadows creeping across the room. Shadows gray and deep. As deep as Ma's ignorance.

"The darkness deepens: Lord, with me abide. . . ."

Shadows filtering through the drawn blind. Rosie tight-lipped and officious. Sonny. Jim, who had left his white wife at home. Pointedly ignoring Mavis, speaking in hushed tones to the florid man in the doorway. Mavis a small inconspicuous brown figure in the corner. The only other brown face in the crowded dining room besides Ma. Even the Old Woman was paler in death. Ma's friends in the kitchen. A huddled, frightened group around the stove.

"Mavis, why do they tell my friends not to visit me?"

And Mavis had shrugged her shoulders indifferently.

"Please, Mavis, why do they tell my friends not to visit me?"

And Mavis had turned on her.

"Do you want Soufie with her black skin to sit in the dining room? Or Ou-Kaar with his kroeskop? Or Eva or Leuntjie? Do you? Do you want Sonny's wife to see them?

Or the white dirt Rosie picks up? Do you want to shame your children? Humiliate them? Expose their black blood?"

And the Old Woman had blubbered. "I only want my friends to visit. They can sit in the kitchen."

And Mavis had sighed helplessly at the simplicity of the doddering Old Woman and had felt like saying, "And what of my friends, my colored friends? Must they also sit in the kitchen?"

And tears had shot into those milky eyes and the mother had looked even older.

"Mavis, I want my friends to visit me, even if they sit in the kitchen. Please, Mavis, they're all I got."

And now Ma's friends sat in the kitchen, a cowering timid group around the fire, speaking the raw gutteral Afrikaans of the Caledon District. They spoke of Ma and their childhood together. Ou-Kaar and Leuntjie and Eva and Ma. Of the Caledon District, cut off from bustling Cape Town. Where the Moravian mission church was crumbling, and the sweet water ran past Wolfgat, and past Karwyderskraal, and lost itself near Grootkop. And the moon rose rich and yellow from the hills behind Solitaire. And now they sat frightened and huddled around the stove, speaking of Ma. Tant Soufie in a new kopdoek, and Ou-Kaar conspicuous in borrowed yellow shoes, sizes too small. And Leuntjie and Eva.

And in the dining room sat Dadda's relations, singing. Dadda's friends who had ignored Ma while she had lived. Dadda's white friends and relations, and a gloss-eyed Mavis, a Mavis who scratched meaninglessly at her broken thumbnail. And now the singing rose in volume as still more people filed in.

"When other helpers fail, and comforts flee,
Help of the helpless, O abide with me! . . ."

they sang to the dead woman.

Mavis could have helped Ma, could have given the understanding she needed, could have protected Ma, could have tried to stop the petty tyranny. But she had never tried to reason with them. Rosie, Sonny, and Jim. She had never pleaded with them, explained to them that the Old Woman was dying. Her own soul ate her up. Gnawed her inside. She was afraid of their reactions lest they should notice her. Preferred to play a shadow, seen but never heard. A vague entity, part of the furniture. If only they could somehow be aware of her emotions. The feelings bottled up inside her, the bubbling volcano below. She was afraid they might openly say, "Why don't you both clear out and leave us in peace, you bloody black bastards!" She could then have cleared out, should then have cleared out, sought a room in Woodstock or Salt River and have forgotten her frustration. But there was Ma. There was the Old Woman. Mavis had never spoken to them, but had vented her spleen on her helpless mother.

"You sent them to a white school. You were proud of your white brats and hated me, didn't you?"

And the mother had stared with oxlike dumbness.

"You encouraged them to bring their friends to the house, to your house, and told me to stay in the kitchen. And you had a black skin yourself. You hated me, Ma, hated me! And now they've pushed you also in the kitchen. There's no one to blame but you. You're the cause of all this."

And she had tormented the Old Woman, who did not retaliate. Who could not retaliate. Who could not understand. Now she sat tortured with memories as they sang hymns for Ma.

The room assumed a sepulchral appearance. Shadows deepened, gray, then darker. Tears, flowers, handkerchiefs, and dominating everything, the simple, bewildered eyes of Ma. Bewildered even in death. So that Mavis had covered them with two pennies, that others might not see.

"I need Thy presence every passing hour. . . ."

sang Dadda's eldest brother, who sat with eyes tightly shut near the head of the coffin. He had bitterly resented Dadda's marriage to a colored woman. Living in sin! A Loupser married to a Hottentot! He had boasted of his refusal to greet Ma socially while she lived, and he attended the funeral only because his brother's wife had died. This was the second time he had been in the dining room. The first time was Dadda's funeral. And now this. A colored girl—his niece, he believed—sitting completely out of place and saying nothing . . . annoying, most annoying.

"What but Thy Grace can foil the tempter's power . . ."

sang the boy in the Eton collar, whose mother had not quite recovered from the shock that Mr. Loupser had had a colored wife. All sang except Mavis, torturing herself with memories.

"I am going to die, Mavis," those milky eyes had told her a week before, "I think I am going to die."

"Ask your white brats to bury you. You slaved for them."

"They are my children but they do not treat me right."

"Do you know why? Shall I tell you why?" And she had driven home every word with an ugly ferocity. "Because they're ashamed of you. Afraid of you, afraid the world might know of their colored mother!"

"But I did my best for them!"

"You did more than your best, you encouraged them, but you were ashamed of me, weren't you? So now we share a room at the back where we can't be seen. And you are going to die, and your white children will thank God that you're out of the way."

"They are your brothers and sisters, Mavis."

"What's that you're saying?" Mavis gasped, amazed at the hypocrisy. "What's that? I hate them and I hate you! I hate you!"

And the Old Woman had whimpered, "But you are my children, you are all my children. Please, Mavis, don't let me die so?"

"You will die in the back room and be buried from the kitchen!"

"It's a sin, Mavis, it's a sin!"

But they had not buried her from the kitchen. They had removed the table from the dining room and borrowed chairs from the neighbors. And now, while they waited for the priest from Dadda's church, they sang hymns.

"Heaven's morning breaks, and earth's vain shadows flee: . . ."

sang the boy in the Eton collar.

"In life and death, O Lord, abide with me! . . ."

the florid man sang loudly, to end the verse. There was an expectant bustle at the door, and then the priest from Dadda's church, St. John the Divine, appeared. All now crowded into the dining room, those who were making wreaths, and Tant Soufie holding Ou-Kaar's trembling hand.

"Please, Mavis, ask Father Josephs at the mission to bury me."

"Ask your brats to fetch him themselves. See them ask a black man to bury you!"

"Please, Mavis, see that Father Josephs buries me!"

"It's not my business, you fool! You did nothing for me!"

"I am your mother, my girl," the Old Woman had sobbed, "I raised you."

"Yes, you raised me, and you taught me my place! You took me to the mission with you, because we were too black to go to St. John's. Let them see Father Josephs for a change. Let them enter our mission and see our God."

And Ma had not understood but whimpered, "Please, Mavis, let Father Josephs bury me."

So now the priest from Dadda's church stood at the head of her coffin, sharp and thin, clutching his cassock with his left hand, while his right held an open prayer book.

"I said I will take heed to my ways: that I offend not in my tongue. I will keep my mouth as it were with a bridle: while the ungodly is in my sight."

Mavis felt the cruel irony of the words.

"I held my tongue and spake nothing. I kept silent, yea even from good words but it was pain and grief to me. . . ."

The fat lady stroked her son's head and sniffed loudly.

"My heart was hot within me, and while I was thus musing the fire kindled, and at the last I spake with my tongue . . ."

Mavis now stared entranced at her broken fingernail. The words seared, and filling, dominated the room.

It was true. Rosie had consulted her about going to the mission and asking for Father Josephs, but she had turned on her heel without a word and walked out into the streets, and walked and walked. Through the cobbled streets of older Cape Town, up beyond the mosque in the Malay quarter on the slopes of Signal Hill. Thinking of the dead woman in the room.

A mother married to a white man and dying in a back room. Walking the streets, the Old Woman with her, followed by the Old Woman's eyes. Eating out her soul. Let them go to the mission and see our God. Meet Father Josephs. But they had gone for Dadda's priest, who now prayed at the coffin of a broken colored woman. And the back room was empty.

"I heard a voice from heaven, Saying unto me, Write, From henceforth blessed are the dead which die in the Lord; even so saith the Spirit; for they rest from their labors. . . ."

"Lord, take Thy servant, Maria Wilhelmina Loupser, into Thy eternal care. Grant her Thy eternal peace and understanding. Thou are our refuge and our rock. Look kindly upon her children who even in this time of trial and suffering look up to Thee for solace. Send

Thy eternal blessing upon them, for they have heeded Thy commandment which is 'Honour thy father and thy mother, that thy days may be long. . . .' "

Mavis felt hot, strangely, unbearably hot. Her saliva turned to white heat in her mouth and her head rolled drunkenly. The room was filled with her mother's presence, her mother's eyes, body, soul. Flowing into her, filling every pore, becoming one with her, becoming a living condemnation.

"Misbelievers!" she screeched hoarsely. "Liars! You killed me! You murdered me! Hypocrites! Don't you know your God!"

ECHOES

by Alf Wannenburgh

THREE MEN STOOD in the dust and looked up at the road sign.

"In two days we shall be in our home country," said Tsolo.

Tsolo, Maki, and Temba had been many days on the road to the Valley of a Thousand Hills. During the day they walked in the yellow dirt beneath the sun, and at night they lighted their fires beside the road and allowed their weariness to drain into the thirsting earth. They spoke little, for the horror of the place they had left remained with them.

More than four hundred of their fellow miners had died in the disaster, and after three weeks of vain efforts to reach those who had been cut off from them by the fall of rock, a funereal quiet had fallen over the workings. The silent, the sullen, the weeping, the bewildered wives and relatives, who had pressed around the fence, had gone, and in their place torn newspapers were impaled on the wire barbs by the wind. The silent winding gear cut a stark silhouette against the gray sky, and the activity of the compound became the despairing preparation for departure of a refugee transit camp.

"The heat of this sun is heavy on our shoulders, like the burden of the white man's laws," said Tsolo, freeing his arms and dropping his pack in the dust at his feet.

"Or like the suffering of our people at the mine," said Maki.

"There are some things we shall not speak of," said Tsolo. "We will change the laws of the white man, but the suffering at the mine can never be changed."

For a moment they were silent because it was with sadness that they remembered the suffering at the mine.

"Let us stay here for the night so that we shall be strong for the walk tomorrow," said Temba.

"No, rather we should walk through the night, because then we shall be home tomorrow evening," said Maki. "Now that I am almost home, my legs are strong and know no tiredness."

"We *will* stay here," said Tsolo.

He led the way through a break in the fence, and they followed him into the deeply etched, dry riverbed.

And that was the way it had always been. Tsolo was

the leader. When they had been at home together, it was Tsolo who had led them to plough; and when the inadequate soil had become poor and the crops had failed, they had followed him to the labor-recruiting office. Once they had even followed him to prison. But that had been a long time ago. His will was the strongest. And that was the way it had always been.

"This is a good place," said Tsolo, dropping his blankets in the sand at the foot of the steep bank.

"It would be better if we went where the river turns, and where we cannot be seen from the road," said Maki. "In this place there is danger!"

There was a silence, and then his voice returned: "There is danger . . . is danger . . . danger . . ."

"Who is it that mocks us!" said Maki.

"It is a trick of the hills," Tsolo replied.

Temba placed his blanket roll firmly beside that of Tsolo. "This is a good place," he agreed.

So they sat for a while in the fading warmth of the sand and watched the shadow of the bank creep across the riverbed.

It was Tsolo who spoke first: "Do you remember that we came through a fence to get here?"

"Yes," said Temba. "It was you who found the opening for us."

"And what does it mean that we came through a fence?"

"It means that we are on the land of a white farmer."

"Now, if I tell you that my stomach is making the rumbling sounds of hunger?"

"Then I would say that on a farm such as this there are sheep."

"Ah! you are a good fellow, Temba. How shall I say . . .? A good fellow," Tsolo said, slapping Temba on the back. "Yes, a *very* good fellow."

Temba felt good. "It is from you that I have learnt these things," he said.

Their talk sounded faintly in the background of Maki's thoughts. He thought of the joy of the home-coming that was before him, and the sorrow of the place that lay behind him; of his escape from the falling rocks that had entombed the miners, and of the talk that it had happened because of the white mine owners, those who had not provided for their safety. He thought too of his friend, Moses—yes, Moses—who had lost his life in the disaster only two days before he was due to leave the mine, two days before he was to return to his family. Only two days. Of how happy he had been, and of the laughter in his eyes when he had spoken of his home. And then there had been a sound like the report of a great gun, and the ceiling of the mine had fallen on his dreams.

Then he remembered the first few days when they had labored with hope, and the many days that followed, when they struggled to clear the broken earth without hope.

But mostly he thought of home, and of the anxious period of waiting, while those who were returning to Mozambique boarded their trains, when the three of them knew that their wives would have heard of the sadness that had come to the mine and would worry for their safety. Then they had been told that they would have to wait a further two weeks for transport to their home country, and Tsolo had rolled up his blankets and spoken. And they had followed him.

"He is a dreamer, this Maki," said Tsolo.

"Yes, and a fool, for when we speak of sheep, we are speaking of *food*," said Temba.

"You want me to worry with food when my mind is filled with much bigger things," said Maki. "In two days I shall be home with my wife. My son will ask me to tell him stories of the things I have seen. We shall sit beside the fire, and then I shall tell him of the painful things that I have seen. In being with my family there is far greater pleasure than in answering the squeals of my stomach. Am I, therefore, a dreamer?"

"What you have learnt of life is like nothing!" said Tsolo. "You have learnt to cut coal and to dream, but you have learnt no wisdom." He spoke with the bitter dust of the road in his voice.

"We cannot live on dreams," said Temba.

"You speak of *home*," said Tsolo. "But what is this home if it is not a patch of poor soil on which our families must starve if we do not find work on the mines so that we can send money to our children? And you speak of this home as if it were Heaven! You are a dreamer, just like the one at the mine who was called Moses."

"Yes, you are like Moses!" shouted Temba.

And the hills repeated: "You are like Moses . . . are like Moses . . . like Moses . . ."

"I do not like this place," said Maki. "We should leave, for even the hills mock us for this talk of stealing sheep when we should be on the road."

"Ah! so now our dreamer is afraid of an echo," jeered Temba.

"Come," said Tsolo. "Let us leave him to his dreams or his fears. There is *men's* work for us to do."

"But why should we do this thing now when we are so near to home?" said Maki. "We may be caught, and then it will be many days before we can continue on our path. These farmers fear us because they are ignorant of us. This fear sometimes causes them to do terrible things to us."

"I have my knife ready, let us find a sheep," said Temba.

"Yes, then let us go," said Tsolo. "Maki, you will make the fire for us while we are gone."

"If we are caught, it will be many days!" he shouted after them as they moved beyond the lip of the bank.

And they did not reply. But the hills answered: "It will be many days . . . be many days . . . many days . . ."

Then darkness and silence came to the bed of the river, and the cold breeze of solitude was chill upon him. Beyond the towering blackness of the opposite bank, filtered light from an invisible moon wove the fabric of the sky with blue threads. He gathered the driftwood of a long-past flood, and heaped it against a boulder in the sandy center of the place where the stream had been.

In the warmth of the flames he felt the companionship of his family. If he excluded all else, the dancing yellow forms created about him the walls of his hut, the gentle love of his wife, and he heard the thirsty questions of his son beside him. And he planned how he would tell him of the many long roads he had traversed to be with him.

"And *still* he is dreaming!" the voice of Tsolo scorned from out of the dark.

Maki shook himself free of his thoughts as the two figures stepped into the light: first Tsolo, carrying the knife, and then Temba, with the carcasss of a sheep slung over his shoulder.

"Ha!" said Temba. "He has not even watched the fire well. Must it also die?"

"Take this," said Tsolo, handing Maki the knife. "We men have done our work. Now it is for the one with the heart of a woman to prepare the sheep for the cooking."

"But if we are found with the blood of this sheep on our hands, we shall not reach home!" said Maki.

"Must we not eat if we are to have strength for the journey tomorrow?" said Temba.

93

"You *dream* of danger—there is no one here," jeered Tsolo.

And the hills confirmed: "There is no one here . . . is no one here . . . no one here . . ."

With the knife in his hand, Maki stood erect before the glowing coals. "My strength does not come from that which belongs to other men," he said.

Tsolo became angry. "Do we not cut coal so that they become rich? Do we not build roads so that they can drive on them, while we must walk? Has not everything that they have been taken from us? You worry because we take this sheep. They have taken all from us—even our strength."

"But I am already strong," shouted Maki, "because I am almost home!"

From the bank above them came a challenge and the sharp crack of a shotgun.

Tsolo and Temba fled from the light and vanished into the blackness where the river turned out of sight of the road.

Just beyond the ragged circle of firelight, illuminated by the weakening flare, lay three bundles of blankets, and beside the fire, two crumpled heaps: the sheep and Maki.

And the hills mocked: "I am almost home . . . am almost home . . . almost home. . . ."

THE PORTABLE RADIO

by James Matthews

HE GAZED MOROSELY at the shopwindows as he slouched along the pavement, his feet kicking at small objects in front of him. He stopped at a large window displaying furniture in a modern bedroom setting.

As he looked at the luxurious bed with its warm, downy blankets, he could imagine himself sinking into its yielding softness and covering himself with its warmth. He thought of his own bare room and reached out a hand to scratch himself where one of his bedfellows was having a late breakfast.

He could still hear the mean voice of his aunt when he told her of the insects sharing his bed. Her voice turned into a screech as she berated him.

"If it wasn't that you are my sister's boy, the streets would have had you a long time ago. Here I'm getting old trying to run a respectable house and you not raising a hand to help me. Job after job the white people give you, but work you won't. If you want your room clean, you do it yourself!"

He grimaced as he relived the scene. He moved nearer to the window, his attention centered on the bed. It was built with a shelf that ran across the head to the floor on both sides. The shelf was filled with books, and a portable radio took pride of place within reach of a reclining figure.

He leaned against the window and closed his eyes. It felt good. The warm blankets enfolded him and filled him with sensuous languor. He reached out a hand and switched on the radio on the shelf above his head, his fingers caressing the protruding knobs. He twisted one and moved from station to station like a bee in search of pollen, leaving a wake of news and music. Settling on one, he leaned back to enjoy the melody.

A rude voice threw him out of paradise. "Look! Would you mind getting away from the window?"

The smug face and cleanliness of the white man made him wince inwardly. His own shirt was in such a condition that if he were to pass a laundry at less than five yards, the collar would drop off. He walked, saddened.

"Anything we could offer you?" "Shoes for the family?" "Something for the house?" The voices of the shop assistants posted in front of their doors rang out for the benefit of the people passing. None of them had a word or spared him a glance as he walked past.

Sometimes he wished he had a steady job, but he knew
it could never be. Some time ago, a very long time ago,
he had had a job, but he could not stick it. The regular
hours were too confining. The large office had been filled
with sunshine and pretty white girls in whose presence he
always felt embarrassed. The sunshine he did not mind,
but the women in their freshly starched frocks, bare-armed
and smelling of lily of the valley, always made him acutely
aware of them. Each time he passed or stood in front of
them he broke into a cold sweat and could not resist looking at the curve of their breasts and the joggle of their
tightly packed buttocks as they walked. He felt out of
place amongst such an abundance of fresh femininity, and
whenever he was sent out on an errand he would drop into
a bar along the way for a glass of wine, and when the day
ended he would be in a happy mood and smile at them
when they bade him good night.

They sacked him when they discovered that, while
drunk, he had forgotten to post a batch of important
letters given earlier in the week. After that he lost
job after job for the same reason. He drifted into casual
work and the little money he received for it was spent
on wine, and despite his aunt's pleading and ranting, he
did not stop his drinking.

He scarcely looked at the windows he passed. The
trouble with his aunt was a thing of the past. Even his
objectionable bedfellows were of no importance. His
mind was filled with the portable radio he had seen. The

richness of its color, its gleaming plastic covering, the long shiny aerial, and the music he could get from it at will. Even the thought of wine was not strong enough to distract his mind from it.

His foot kicked against something heavy, the heel of his shoe dragging it along. The weight of the object shifted the last nail that held the heel secure. He stared with dismay at the heel, which peeped back at him from the side of the shoe.

A small tobacco pouch was next to the heel.

His nerves tensed like a pointer spotting his quarry. He moved back to the wall and dragged the pouch with his foot. He scratched his calf nonchalantly. A few more scratches and the pouch was in his hand.

His fingers flowed over the unyielding surface. He was puzzled. The contents could not be tobacco; it was too bulky, and he could feel the sharp edges. Covering the pouch from observant eyes, he undid the top. The greenness of banknotes wrapped around some object was revealed. With a furtive movement he slipped the pouch into his pocket and walked in the direction of his home.

He kept his hand on the pouch lest its contents disappear like some crazy dream. He was deliriously happy and felt like doing a dance on the pavement, but a policeman on the corner decided him against it. The policeman might not understand his feeling and arrest him for being drunk. With what he had in his pocket, he was not taking any chances.

Running the gantlet of his aunt's sharp tongue, he made for his room. A glance showed that his aunt had made her usual search for concealed liquor. Making sure the door was bolted, he drew the pouch from his pocket and spilled its contents on the table, his fingers rubbing lovingly against it. He unwrapped the banknotes from the object they covered and saw that it was four half crowns.

There were eight five-pound notes. He arrayed them in a line, then changed the pattern. He made four piles and placed a half crown on each pile. He lingered on their greenness. Forty pounds. A fortune.

A sound came from the doorway. He grabbed the money and shoved it in his pocket. He walked on tiptoe to the door and with one swift movement drew the bolt and swung it open.

His aunt was framed in the doorway like Cupid in the act of releasing an arrow.

"Why do you lock the door? If it's wine you brought into your room, you can just carry it out again. It's sick I am of the mess you make."

"It's not wine I have," he replied in a meek voice.

"Remember what I told you this morning." With this last threat she waddled her way along the passage, the staircase protesting as she shifted her weight from foot to foot.

He searched his pockets for a stub of pencil, and on the

back of the calendar that served also as a decoration, he worked out his fortune.

He had more than enough to pay for the portable. He looked at himself in the mirror. He would have to buy something to wear first or else they might refuse to serve him. The white man with the smug face was not likely to let him pass the door without asking many questions.

His aunt was working in the kitchen; he could hear the banging of pots. Silently he crept down the stairs and out of the house.

He went to the secondhand shop where most of the neighborhood bought their clothing. It also served as a clearing house for those with goods to sell.

He selected a white linen suit, a pair of canvas shoes, and a pale blue shirt. He was drawn to a rattan cane above which hung a cheap panama hat. He could not resist the temptation and bought the lot, adding a blue and white candy-striped tie. On his way out he spotted a blanket, made a rapid calculation, and bought it. With the generosity of the newly rich, he threw the sixpence change to the boy helping in the shop.

His aunt saw him before he could mount the stairs.

"Hey! What's that you've got under your arm?" She eyed the bulky parcel with suspicion.

He took some money out of his pocket and gave her a pound. "I've had some luck, Auntie. Buy yourself a present."

She stood contemplating the money in her hand, and before she could speak, he was past her and climbing the steps to his room. She murmured something and put the money into the large pocket of the apron encasing her ample bosom.

He stood at the top of the stairs and called for hot water with which to shave. After some delay, his aunt pulled her bulk up the stairs. With a baleful glare she slammed the container on the table, splashing the water, which she wiped off with the edge of her apron.

A hot bath and a shave later, he emerged resplendent in his new suit, with the panama hat dipped at a jaunty angle. With a twirl of his cane he walked down the stairs. His milky teeth lit up his brown face as he walked past his speechless aunt. "I'll be back in an hour or so," he said.

As he walked down Waterkant Street, each shop he passed had its attendant seeking his custom.

The salesman did not recognize him when he entered the shop.

"What can I do for you, sir?"

He did not reply at once, savoring the servility of the salesman. He looked at a table and four padded chairs. Picking up a reading lamp, he watched the salesman hovering nearby. He turned toward him.

"I want to buy a portable radio."

"Step this way, sir. I will be glad to show you our

latest models." The salesman was like a cat confronted with a cup of cream. He was almost purring with pleasure.

He stood with affected boredom as if buying a radio set was a tiresome procedure.

The salesman flitted from set to set, twisting knobs, pulling out aerials, sending forth a blare of music with a twist of the wrist, praising one set for its color scheme and another for its durability.

He occupied himself with an imaginary speck of dust on his coat, carefully flicking it away with a large cotton handkerchief, which he folded in a triangle and replaced in his breast pocket.

His choice was narrowed down to two sets. He had to choose between the glitter of one and the durability of the other. He held back. The portable with its shiny surface would surely raise him in the estimation of his aunt, but on the other hand, the second set could be played by battery and when exhausted could be converted to electricity.

The salesman was silent, hardly daring to breathe lest he disturb the fish nibbling at the hook. He took the one with the battery.

His aunt followed him into the room. Placing the portable on the table, he told her to close her eyes while he undid the wrapping. Reluctantly she complied with his request. He laughed as her face broke into pieces at the sight of the portable. Using all the technical terms he could remember, he explained to her how it worked and its advantages.

Work was forgotten while his aunt shared with him the hours of listening to the music. Even news reports were listened to with careful attention.

Dressed in his finery, he spent the days holding court in the bar on the corner and at night he would return swaying ever so slightly, and with the smell of wine on his breath. His aunt overlooked it all, and a plate of hot food awaited him each night.

In the dim glow of his room, and covered by the extra warmth of his new blanket, he would ease back, stroking the soft surface of the blanket while the music flowed over him in waves of contentment.

His aunt tolerated him even when his drinking bouts became more frequent and lasted longer, until finally he had no more money left.

The panama hat and rattan cane were the first to go. They brought him enough to buy a bottle of wine. He held on to the suit as long as he could, but his thirst was too strong. The secondhand dealer stood with a complacent air as he handed the money over.

He was too dispirited to argue and walked listlessly from the store. Around his neck was the candy-striped tie, curling at the edges but still making a brave attempt to strike a gay note, making him look like a discarded Christmas tree. His canvas shoes completed the picture, adding a smell of their own.

He walked home with the two bottles of wine he had bought at the off-sales next to the bar, ignoring the pleas from his former courtiers.

He placed the two bottles on the table and switched on the portable. The indicator showed no bright gleam. He tried it again with the same result, and then it dawned on him that the electricity was cut off. He turned a knob at the back of the portable and converted it to battery. When he switched it on, the indicator jumped to life and music rushed forth.

When his aunt entered the room, she glared at him. The wine had removed his fear of her. "You forgot about the batteries." His voice ended in a giggle. She slammed the door.

He took off his shoes and fell back on the bed with a bottle near at hand.

A roar of music woke him the next morning. His throat was dry; next to the bed stood the remaining bottle, which he opened and held up, the wine trickling from the side of his mouth.

The continuous playing soon drained the batteries of the portable and he spent miserable days cooped in his room.

Through the window he could see the time on the Foundery's clock. It would be a good four hours before his aunt would switch on the lights. He stretched himself out on the bed and tried to sleep.

When he awoke, the light streaming from beneath the

door told him that it was time to switch on the portable.

He fiddled around with the dial, trying each wave band in turn. He tuned in to stations he never knew existed.

Brazil called with the throb of drums pounding out a South American rhythm that jerked his body alive. Mexico contributed a fiesta, bringing to mind a vision of pretty señoritas and gay caballeros strumming guitars and dancing a fandango. The plaintive wail of a clarinet moaning "The Birth of the Blues" welcomed him to America.

He turned it on to its full volume, the music flooding his room and spilling out into the passage, rolling downstairs until it filled the house.

The music was a drug and it soothed him.

In the midst of its healing it was suddenly snatched away as the lights went off in the passage. He looked at the portable and then grabbed it by its sides and shook it violently. From outside the door his aunt called him. "See how you like it. I've had enough of you. I've turned off the light and tomorrow you clear out of here and take that damn box of noise with you." Then she laughed. Louder, ever louder, until it seemed that the now silent portable had somehow been transplanted inside her. "Hee-hee, haw-haw," her laughter lashed, sending him cringing beneath the blankets with his fingers pressed into his ears. "Hee-hee, haw-haw," it rumbled about him. He flung the blankets aside and grabbed the portable, raised it overhead and smashed it against the wall. "Hee-hee, haw-haw, ho-ho-ho," it was still present, stronger, louder, a dynamo of diabolical merriment. "Hee-hee, haw-haw, ho-ho-ho," the peals of laughter made his body writhe.

Eyes glazed, he took hold of an empty wine bottle and smashed its top on the edge of the table and crept quietly from the room to silence the "Hee-hee, haw-haw, ho-ho-ho" that threatened to tear him to shreds.

SLIPPER SATIN
by Alex La Guma

THE STREET couldn't have changed much in four months. The same two rows of houses were there, with their fenced stoops and verandas; the same Indian grocery shop, and the back of the warehouse that had a big sign painted across the whole expanse of wall. There were the same gray pavements, cracked in places. Perhaps the paint and color-wash on the houses had faded and peeled somewhat during the four months, and there were wide streaks down the wall of the warehouse, damaging the big black lettering.

And the people were there, too. The little knots of twos and threes at the gates of some of the houses, the row of idle men against the warehouse wall, and the children playing in the gutters. Nothing had really changed in the street.

She stared straight ahead as she came into the street, but sensed the wave of interest that stirred the people. Recognition tapped them on the shoulder and she felt the faces turning toward her. There was a little flurry among the group at one gate, or at a fence, and then it ran on quickly and mysteriously to the next, and the next, down the street, so that the women peered slyly at first, murmuring among themselves, watching her approach, and then breaking into loud chatter when she had passed.

"That is she . . . that's she . . ."

"Got four months, mos', for immorality . . ."

"Come home again, hey? We don't want damn whores on this street."

And the needle-sharp eyes followed her all the way, suspicious, angry, and secretly happy, too, that there was another victim for the altars of their gossiping.

With the men it was different. They watched her come, some openly, some from under the rims of their lowered eyelids, watching her and smiling gently at the thought of her conquest. Who the hell cared if it had been a white boy? He had been lucky enough, hadn't he? A man didn't begrudge another that kind of victory, even if it had been across the line. A man was a man, and a girl a girl. She was still around, anyway, so maybe there was a chance for one of them.

They were amused at the stupid malice of the women-folk and they showed their defiance by saying, "Hullo, Myra. How you, Myra? Nice to see you again, Myra. How you keeping, Myra?" And they felt the stares of the women, too, and grinned at the girl to show that it was okay with them.

She smiled gently, hearing their voices, but kept her head up and her eyes forward. But she felt the bitterness inside her like a new part of her being. She had finished with crying, and crying had left the bitterness behind like the layer of salt found in a pan after the water had evaporated. So that even as she smiled there was a scornful twist to her mouth.

She was tall and brown and good-looking, with the fullness of lips, the width of cheekbone, the straight nose and firm chin, and the blue eyes that she had inherited from the intermarriage of her ancestors generations past. Her body was firm, a little hardened from hard work for four months, but still beautiful; the breasts full and wide at the bases, the belly flat and the thighs and legs long and shapely.

She reached the house at last and climbed the steps onto the veranda. When she opened the front door the smell of cooking came to her from the kitchen at the end of the passageway. The old smell of frying onions and oil.

She walked down the passage and there was the elderly woman, her mother, standing over the pots on the black iron stove, short and stout, with thinning hair tied in a knot at the back of her head.

Myra leaned against the jamb of the kitchen door, a small panic struggling suddenly inside her. But she fought it off and said, casually, "Hullo, Ma."

Her mother looked around with a jerk, a big stirring-spoon, poised over a saucepan, in the thick, scrubbed hand that shook a little. Myra looked into the decaying, middle-aged eyes and saw the surprise replaced slowly by hardness, the twist of the elderly mouth, the deep lines in the throat and neck and the network of wrinkles.

"Oh. So you're back. Back with your shame and disgrace, hey?"

"I'm back, Ma," Myra said.

"You brought disgrace on us," her mother said harshly, the spoon waving in the girl's face. "We all good and decent people, but you brought us shame." The face crumbled suddenly and tears seeped out of the eyes. "You brought us shame. You couldn't go and pick a boy of your own kind, but you had to go sleep with some white loafer. You brought us shame, after how I worked and slaved to bring you up. Nobody ever been to jail in our family, and you a girl, too. It's enough to give an old woman a stroke, that's what it is."

Myra gazed at her mother and pity edged its way forward at the sight of a work-heavy body, the ruined face, the tears, but something else thrust pity aside and she said steadily, "It wasn't any disgrace, Ma. It's no disgrace to love a man, no matter what color he is or where he comes from. He was nice and he wasn't what you call a white loafer. He would have married me if he could. He always said so."

"What's the matter with your own kind of people? What's the matter with a nice colored boy?" The quavering voice sobbed and hiccoughed and the girl felt a pang of revulsion.

"There's nothing wrong with colored boys," she said, more in irritation than anger. "Nobody said there was anything wrong with colored boys. I happened to fall for a white boy, that's all."

"It's no better than being a whore," the old woman sobbed. "No better than that."

"All right," the girl said bitterly. "I'm no better than a whore. All right. Leave it like that. I'm a whore and I brought you disgrace. Now then."

"Don't you talk to your own ma like that!" The old woman began to shout angrily, waving the spoon about. "You got a cheek to talk to your poor ma like that, after all I done for you. You haven't got respek, that's what. Got no respek for your betters. There's your sister Adie getting married soon. To a nice boy of her own kind. Not like you. Getting married and a fine example you are for her. You. You. Yes, you."

"I'm glad Adie's getting married," Myra said with forced dryness. "I hope to God her husband takes her away to go and live on their own."

"You haven't got no respek, talking to your mother that way. Just shows what kind you are. Adie at least been supporting me while you been in that disgrace, in that jail for four months. And now you just come to bring bad luck into the house. You bad luck, that's what you are."

Myra smiled a little scornfully and said, "All right, I'm a whore and a disgrace and bad luck. All right, Ma. But don't worry. You won't starve with me around."

"If you get a job," the mother snapped. "And if I was a boss I wouldn't give no damn whore a job."

"Oh, stop it, Ma. You'll make yourself sick."

"Ja. And whose fault will that be?"

Myra looked at the hysterical old woman for a second and then turned away. She felt like crying, but she was determined not to. She'd had enough of crying. She left the old woman and turned into the room off the passageway.

It was still the same room, with the wardrobe against one wall and the dressing table between the two single beds where she and her sister Ada slept. She lay down on her bed in her clothes and stared at the ceiling.

Ada getting married. She was genuinely glad about that. She and Ada had always been very close. She thought, no Mixed Marriages Act and no Immorality Act and maybe I'd be getting married, too, but you got four months in jail instead of a wedding. Poor old Tommy.

She began to wonder whether Tommy really had been

serious about loving her. No, he must have been. He really had been. He had loved her, but it must have proved too much for him. But what did he have to go and do that for? If he had loved her that bad he would have stuck it out, no matter what. Maybe Tommy just couldn't see any other way. So that night when the police had come in on them he'd gone from the bedroom into the living room and to his desk, and before they knew anything about it he had the little automatic pistol out of the drawer and had shot himself.

So that was that. Poor Tommy. Maybe he thought it was a disgrace, too. Maybe he thought that, in spite of all his love. But she didn't care any more.

She lay on the bed and tried not to think about it. She thought about Ada instead. She would like to give Ada a nice wedding present. She wouldn't go to the wedding ceremony, of course. She'd save the dear old family the embarrassment. But she'd have to give Ada a nice wedding present.

And then in the middle of her thoughts the front door banged, feet hurried along the passageway, and the door opened and there was Ada.

"Myra. Myra, ou pal. You're back."

Her younger sister was there, flinging bag and jacket aside, and hugging her. "I heard those damn old hens up the street cackling about my sister, and I just ran all the way."

"Hullo, Adie. Good to see you again. Give me a kiss.

Yes, I think they'll be cackling a long time still." She added bitterly, "The old woman feels the same."

"Don't you worry, bokkie. Hell, I'm glad you're back for the wedding."

"How's the boy friend?"

"Okay." Ada grinned at her sister. "He doesn't give a damn. His family had things to say, of course. But I've got him like that." She showed a fist, laughing. "He'll listen to Adie, family or no family."

"You got everything ready?"

"Oh, yes. The wedding dress will be ready the end of the week, on time for Saturday. I managed to save and bought some stuff for the house. Joe put in for one of those Council cottages and they said we can move in."

"I'll miss you."

"Garn. You can mos' come and visit us any time. Listen, if you like I could talk to Joe about you coming to stay with us. What do you say?"

"No. You go off on your own and be happy. I'll stay on here. Me and Ma will maybe fight all the time, but I'll manage."

"What you going to do, Myra?"

"Don't know," Myra told her. "The old lady will need looking after. Say, have you really got everything?"

"Oh, yes. Except maybe the frock to change into next Saturday night. I'll have to wear the wedding dress right through the whole business. I did see the damn nicest

114

party frock at the Paris Fashions, but I suppose I'll have
to do without a change on Saturday night. It's so lousy
having to wear the wedding dress at the party, too.
Things and stuff might spill onto it. The bride ought to
change for the evening celebrations. We're having a
party at Joe's place. I thought it'd be grand to have a
dress to change into, though. But I worked out every
penny, so I won't be able to afford eight guineas. Such
nice darn slipper satin, too. Real smart."

Ada got up from the edge of the bed and started re-
moving her work clothes. "Tell me, Myra, was it bad up
there?"

"Not too bad. I did washing most of the time. But I
don't want to talk about it, man."

"We won't," Ada smiled, struggling into black stove-
pipe jeans. "That's all finished and done with. Now you
just take it easy and I'll call you when supper's ready.
You like some tea?"

"Thanks."

Ada grinned and ducked out of the room, leaving
Myra alone again on the single bedstead. Dear old Ada,
with a whore for a sister. The old woman would prob-
ably say it would be bad luck to have me coming visiting
them. She felt sorry for her mother, for Ada, for all those
women up the street, for Tommy. Poor old Tommy.
Tommy couldn't stand up to it. Him and his love. Him
and his I love you. She had died, too, she thought, the

instant Tommy pulled the trigger. Poor old Tommy. She felt sorry for all of them.

She thought, Adie is going to be happy. She wanted Adie to be happy and she told herself that Adie would have that slipper satin dress she wanted, as a present from her. She could earn eight guineas easily.

The Possessed

Surely oppression maketh a wise man mad.
—ECCLESIASTES

THE SNAKE PIT

by Alf Wannenburgh

"Passion fruit, an' not a drop of anything else since
my kiddie died—ask anybody," the little man, wearing a
black tie in a plastic shirt collar, was telling his mate
as Andy and I shouldered our way through the four-
deep lining of day-shift stevedores and crane drivers
around the bar and gave the barman the "I'm thirsty"
sign.

Down the other end of the counter I sighted Mike
and Jim Barton listening with no apparent interest to
some fellow wearing a frayed sports coat and checked
shirt, and Mike nodded to show that he was coming over.
A barman drifted across and sloshed two brandies into
thick sixpenny tumblers for Andy and me, while Andy
looked apathetically at the no-longer-transparent measur-
ing bulbs and stained wine casks.

". . . but I've laid off the pots now, that's for sure—
true's God," the little man was saying.

"What you say they call this place?" asked Andy.

"Snake Pit."

"So—how come?"

". . . must have been mad or something, way I was
carrying on," the little man was saying. "Every night
when I got home, I was full of dike—an' there was my
wife with this little sick kiddie . . . gee, that was a beautiful kiddie, our first . . . an' me drunk as a coot most
times . . ."

"Well, look who's dropped in from the posh pubs—
what brings you here?" The voice and the hand on my
shoulder belonged to Mike.

"Showing Andy around the Cape Town dives. From
Jo'burg—likes slumming." There were introductions from
which the man in the frayed sports coat and checked shirt
was somehow excluded, although he insisted on shaking
hands all the same.

". . . was like a lousy government keeps contaminating
everybody an' mucking up the country. Only, with me
drinking like I was, I was contaminating myself an'
mucking up my wife an' kiddie," the little man was
saying.

"Keen political discussion up at the Grand the other
night," said Mike. "Very high level except for one bloke
kept buggering it up always asking if we wanted our
sisters to marry Kaffirs."

"Good old low-water mark of South African democracy
—to every white-skinned boy of eighteen, the inalienable
right to choose his own brother-in-law," said Andy. And
I remembered that he'd always been rather hot on politics—*red* hot, in fact.

"I'll shoot her! I'll shoot her!" said Jim Barton, stabbing his fist into the counter, and preparing to do the
same with his head.

"Shoot who?" asked Andy.

"Shoot my sister if she marries a Native."

"Oh, Christ! help me—help us all!" said Mike, slapping
his hand to his forehead and reeling in mock despair.

For a moment I was pleased that Andy wasn't a
crusader or missionary or anything like that to waste
his time arguing with the completely lost. I hate the
political jag. Then this unwelcome fellow in the frayed
sports coat and checked shirt just had to go and make his
contribution:

"An' why shouldn't she marry who she likes? There's
some of them what's been to the university an' got
degrees an' things, an' . . ."

A possible convert! I'd forgotten that Andy was a hog
for making converts—when they were easy.

"This is a very famous pub," I started. "All the early
gold and diamond deals . . . you remember Cecil John
Rhodes. I.D.B. . . . even that shooting last month . . ."

But it didn't help, we had lost Andy for the evening.
He moved over towards the fellow in the frayed sports

coat and checked shirt, his right hand extended. The fellow pushed his empty glass in front of Andy, and the barman promptly filled it with tickey hock. Andy paid without a murmur.

"I'm adjourning to the Grand," said Mike. "Hope that marriage guidance chap that's so interested in our sisters isn't there."

Jim Barton followed, mumbling about caliber, velocity, range, and an accumulation of ballistic data he'd been taught when he did his citizen force training.

"Take my advice an' do the same," the little man was saying. "Now I've got me this bookkeeping job in South West, going to get away from all this I'm used to. Make a new start—a new way of life. Owe it to my wife an' other kiddie . . ."

"What's the use running away from it? You'll find the same sort of thing there," his mate was objecting. "Much better you stay an' beat it here, to my mind. Make your new life here, then you can say you've really done something."

"An' the temptations," said the little man. "What about the temptations? First you think you've got things going right, an' then one day you meet an old pal—bang, back where you were, resolutions an' everything gone to hell!"

". . . so I can get them to send you some literature—stuff to read—that will help you," Andy was saying, as he wrote his new friend's name and address into a little black notebook.

The friend was nodding and edging his empty glass in front of Andy, while a barman unscrewed the cap of a tickey hock bottle.

"Not that I don't love this place—suppose I do, really. Only thing is I'd like to know if I was doing the right thing by my wife an' kiddie if I stayed," the little man was saying.

"If you are willing, an' have the strength to change your whole way of life, then you can't miss," said his mate.

Andy was quizzing his new friend: "So, what sort of society do we live in?"

"Multiracial."

"But our democracy must be . . .?"

"Nonracial."

"And that means . . .?"

"Equal right for all, an' my sister can marry who she likes."

"Have you any friends who think the same way as you?" Andy was trembling with the excitement of his discovery. "Maybe we can get together and have a little . . ."

"Yes, I suppose I have," said the new friend, tendering his empty glass for consideration. "But there's still one thing I'll like to as' you first. Will you let a Native come an' sit in *here* with you?"

"Good heavens, of course yes! I mean to say, if . . ."

"Well, not me. 'S okay what my sister does, long as she

doesn't bring him home to my place, but I'm not going to have them coming an' sitting in here with me—*wasn't brought up that way!*"

Then, as he presented his glass more insistently, Andy grabbed me by the arm and pulled me out into the street. Turning me around, he looked up at the red and white sign that clashed with the mellowed maturity of the teak door:

S. A. Railways
Wine Buffet
Whites Only

The little man with the black tie in the plastic shirt collar had followed us into the street, and he paused beside us to see what we were looking at.

"*What* did you say they called this place?" asked Andy. "Snake Pit."

Andy didn't ask me why, he just smiled as if he understood.

"Saw a fil-m called *The Snake Pit* once," mumbled the little man. "Was 'bout a madhouse."

NO ROOM
AT SOLITAIRE

by Richard Rive

NOW FANIE VAN DER MERWE had every right to be annoyed. Here he stood, owner of the only hotel in Solitaire, wiping glasses in an empty bar on Christmas Eve. The owner of the only canteen till Donkergat, and facing empty tables and chairs. Well, not quite empty, because old Dawie Volkwyn sat sullen and morose at the counter. But then Dawie Volkwyn always sat sullen and morose at the counter. Fanie couldn't remember when Dawie had not sat on the very same stool opposite the kitchen door. To have the only canteen for miles around empty on Christmas Eve.

It was obviously done for spite. Oom Sarel always did things for spite. Take the case of Marietjie Louw when she went out with Dawie. His argument with Fanie had started with politics. Oom Sarel had sat at the counter, the way he always sat, holding forth on every subject. God's gift to South African politics, Fanie had mumbled under his breath. Fanie had kept calm until Oom Sarel had said that Kaffirs could not be educated beyond Std. II. Fanie had been annoyed, very annoyed, and had quoted the case of Witbooi's cousin. Now Witbooi's cousin had reached Std. VI at a school in Cape Town. Oom Sarel had insisted that it was unheard of, and if it were so it was deliberately done by the missionaries or the English or something like that. Fanie had added that Witbooi's cousin could read and write in Afrikaans even better than some of the white bywoners. Oom Sarel had become very red about the neck and had said he would not drink in a bar owned by a Communist. Then he had walked out. Now many had walked out before, but Oom Sarel was different. He owned Bo-Plaas, the richest maize farm in the District, and had already been to Johannesburg twice and sometimes visited Hermanus in the Cape for his holidays.

So it was obviously done for spite. Otherwise why should Oom Sarel have a Christmas Eve braaivleis and invite everyone in Solitaire except Fanie van der Merwe and, well, and Danie Volkwyn? The free boerewors and brandy were given to lure away all his customers. Louw Viljoen and Daantjie Pretorius and Jan Mostert and them. Fanie would have loved to be there. He would have closed the bar and given Witbooi the evening off. But then, he had been pointedly ignored.

So now he halfheartedly wiped glasses on Christmas Eve and surveyed the deserted canteen. Only Dawie. But then no one ever invited Dawie anywhere. Though in spite of his drinking and bad reputation with women, Dawie Volkwyn knew life. And when he had had sufficient brandy, he would belch, lean back comfortably, narrow his eyes, and hold forth on religion, politics, the English, why the world was going to the dogs, and Marietjie Louw. He was certain that Marietjie was a little more than interested in him, but her father thought Dawie too old at fifty. Marietjie herself must be well over forty, and there was no prospect of a husband in sight.

"Ja, Dawie," said Fanie sitting opposite him, "so goes the world."

Dawie made no reply, so Fanie opened a bottle of brandy and filled two glasses. They drank in silence, each occupied with his own thoughts.

Fanie filled again. "It is hard when there is no business."

Another long silence, while they sipped their brandy. After the third glass Dawie replied.

"I hear Oom Sarel slaughtered two oxen."

"Ja."

"And three lambs, and fowls and geese."

"*Ja.*"

"And Oom Sarel bought all the wine and brandy from Cohen in Donkergat."

"*Ja*," repeated Fanie fatalistically. He began to have serious doubts about the ability of Witbooi's cousin to read and write in Afrikaans. He would have to ask his kitchen boy. Witbooi's cousin was beginning to mess up his business.

"I never could have thought my bar would be empty on Christmas Eve."

"So goes the world."

Fanie poured Dawie another drink.

"Well here's to Christmas. *Veels geluk.*"

"*Veels geluk.*"

"A long time ago in Bethlehem."

"Ja," said Dawie, looking far back in time, far beyond his fifty years. "It was a long time ago."

"But He will return."

"It says so in the Book."

"*Ja.*"

"In Revelations."

"He will come in all His glory."

"And the trumpets shall sound."

"But I've been thinking, Fanie."

"*Ja?*"

"When he first came they didn't know Him."

"So?"

"It stands so in the Book."

"I know."

"How will we know Him when He comes again?"

"You are speaking dangerous things."

"What if He is not a White man?"

"He is a White man!"

"I know," Dawie said weakly.

They slipped back into silence and Fanie automatically refilled the glasses.

"How will we recognize Him?"

"There will be signs, Dawie."

"Like what?"

"It stands in the Book."

Fanie hoped that Louw Viljoen, Jan Mostert, and Daantjie Pretorius would still come in for a quick one, even if Oom Sarel's wine was free. So he bought it from Cohen in Donkergat. Sheer spite.

"Fanie, I'm not a religious man."

"I know, Dawie."

"I'm not a church-going man."

"I know."

"But I like to ask questions."

"Ja."

"How will we know Him when He comes again?"

"It stands in the Book."

"What does it say?"

"You must read it in the Book."

"I'm not a reading man."

"Ja." Fanie felt that the conversation was leading nowhere, and decided to revert to the subject of Witbooi's cousin. "Do you believe Kaffirs can read?"

"I don't know, Fanie."

"If they went to school in Cape Town?"

"Maybe."

"That's what I told Oom Sarel."

"And so?"

"Called me a kaffir-boetie."

"Wragtig."

"And a Communist."

"That is bad."

"So I told him about Witbooi's cousin."

"Ja?"

"You know him?"

"No."

"He passed Std. Vl."

"That can be."

"Then Oom Sarel walked out on me."

Both men moodily sipped at their glasses. Dawie wondered whether Marietjie Louw was also at Bo-Plaas and if she was thinking of him. Fanie hoped Louw Viljoen and Daantjie Pretorius would drop in after the braaivleis. After all he liked Louw.

"Baas."

Louw was argumentative, but one could get on with him.

"Baas!"

"Ja, Witbooi?"

"There is a man with a woman outside who want to see the baas."

"Tell them to come in."

"Baas, they are from my people."

"Tell them to go to hell." He turned back to Dawie. "Kaffirs are becoming more and more cheeky."

"That is true."

"A lazy bunch of good-for-nothings."

"I agree with you."

"But that doesn't mean some can't read and write."

"True."

"In Afrikaans."

"That is so."

"Take Witbooi's cousin."

"Ja. Witbooi's cousin."

The kitchen boy reappeared, greatly agitated.

"Baas, the man say it is serious."

"Chase them away."

"I tried to, baas."

"Tell them I'll come with my shotgun."

"It's no use, baas."

"Get rid of them."

"I try again, baas."

Fanie removed a fresh bottle of brandy from the shelf and removed the tinsel expertly with his teeth. He twisted the corkscrew in and pulled. He refilled the two glasses, feeling much better, even jovial.

"Now take Witbooi's cousin."

"Ja."

"Now there's a clever Kaffir."

"Must be."

"He works in an office in Cape Town."

"Ja?"

"Writes letters for his boss."

"Wragtig!"

"And at the end of the month he sends out accounts."

"Some of these people can do it."

"But Oom Sarel can't understand."

"Oom Sarel is difficult."

Witbooi tapped Fanie lightly on the sleeve.

"Please, baas, come and see."

"What?"

"The man and woman at the back door."

"Didn't you chase them away?"

"I can't, baas."

"Verdomp! Bring my shotgun!"

"Ja, baas."

"Kom, Dawie, let's get rid of them."

Dawie was reluctant to shift from the half-full bottle of brandy, but had to be careful not to annoy Fanie. He climbed unsteadily to his feet and swayed behind the hotelkeeper through the canteen and kitchen.

In the doorway stood a bearded man of an indefinite

age, holding a donkey by a loose rein. A black woman
sat groaning on the stoep.

"Ja?" said Fanie.

"My wife, she is sick."

"So what is wrong?"

"She is sick, baas."

"But what is the matter?"

"She is going to have a child."

"I am not a verdomde midwife."

"I look for a doctor, baas."

"Yes?"

"There is no one in the dorp."

"So what can I do?"

"They all at Bo-Plaas, baas."

"So?"

"I need help, baas, my wife is sick."

"Go to Bo-Plaas."

"She is sick, baas."

"Come on, get away."

"Please, baas."

"Voertsek!" Fanie turned on his heels, followed by
Dawie. They settled down to their disturbed drink.

"As if I'm a verdomde midwife."

"Kaffirs are getting more cheeky."

"They come to me of all people."

"Wragtig."

"I run a hotel, I don't deliver babies."

"That's the worst of these people."

Suddenly Fanie's eyes gleamed with a sadistic delight. "I hope they go to Bo-Plaas."

"Ja."

"That would put Oom Sarel in his place."

"That would."

"And the woman must give birth right there."

"Ja, that would be very funny."

"Please, my baas."

Fanie turned around, annoyed at Witbooi.

"They're still here, baas."

"Huh?"

"They won't go away."

"Chase them."

"They want a place to rest."

"There's no room."

"In one of the shelters, baas."

"There's no place."

"The woman is very sick."

Fanie downed his brandy at one gulp and then drank two more in quick succession. "There's no room!" he repeated, then stared, amazed, at Dawie, who had begun to laugh hysterically in a high-pitched giggle.

"And what do you find so funny?"

"There's no room," Dawie repeated, "no room in the inn."

"And so?"

"Can't you see, man?"

"No."

"It's Christmas Eve."

"Allewereld!"

"The Kaffir had a donkey."

"Ja, ja!" Fanie burst out in a guffaw, but there was a false ring. He choked, spluttered, and then burst into a fit of coughing. He recovered and laughed till the tears streamed down his cheeks. Dawie laughed dutifully.

"No room at the inn."

"Ja, that is very funny."

Fanie was suddenly silent. Dawie stifled a half-hearted attempt to laugh.

"Come, let's go and see," Fanie said suddenly.

"The Kaffir?"

"Ja."

"All right."

"Bring the brandy along."

"And the glasses."

They got up unsteadily and walked to the back door. Fanie looked ash gray under his leathery skin. There was no one at the door.

"Witbooi!"

No reply.

"Witbooi! !"

The servant appeared suddenly, as if from nowhere.

"Baas?"

"Where's the man?"

"I don't know, baas."

"You're lying."

"It's true, baas."

"Where are they?"

"The woman is very sick."

"So where did they go?"

"I put them in the stable, baas."

"Hemelsnaam!"

"Allewereld!"

Fanie and Dawie slowly looked at each other and then, at the same time, timidly looked toward the sky to see whether there was a bright star.

A GLASS OF WINE

by *Alex La Guma*

THAT EVENING we were sitting in the front room
of Ma Schrikker's place when the door opened and this
boy came in. He was tall and young and thin as a billiard
cue, and had beautiful red-gold hair combed in a high
pompadour, and a pink-white skin. He looked very young
and handsome and a little like one of those Johns you see
on the screen.

"Hullo," Arthur said, smiling at the boy. I smiled at
him too, and he nodded and smiled back at us.

We were drinking some of Ma Schrikker's wine and
taking our time about it because we had nowhere else to
go that evening, and besides, we had paid six-and-sixpence
for the bottle. Ma Schrikker didn't mind the customers
taking their time over their drinks as long as the price
was right.

She was fat and dark and jolly and always had a welcome smile for everybody, especially when they were
customers. Although I thought her joviality was stimulated
by anticipation of a rise in sales every time somebody
arrived, because there were times when she was a real
menace.

"How you keeping, pally?" Arthur asked the boy.
He was a little drunk from the red and that made him
friendlier than ever.

"Fine," the boy said shyly. "I'm fine."

"Sit, man. Sit down," Arthur said, still smiling at the
boy.

He sat down on the settee and looked around. He
had been there before, often, but he always looked around
as if he was missing something.

There were a couple of old pictures on the walls—
one of the steamship, and another of the Duke and
Duchess of Windsor cut out of the photogravure section
of a newspaper, framed in black—and a fancy, embroidered frame that had a little house on a hill spotted
by flies, and flowers in the garden and embroidered words
that said *Home Sweet Home.* There was also a big oval
frame of an old John with white whiskers and a come-
to-Jesus collar that Ma Schrikker claimed was her great-
grandfather.

But we all knew the boy wasn't really interested in the
pictures. He'd come to see one of Ma Schrikker's girls,

and looking around was just a sort of embarrassed way
of indicating that.

"Well," Arthur said. "Have a glass of wine, pal."

He picked up the bottle and looked at it in the light.
"There's one more dop over."

"Leave it." The boy smiled. "Don't worry."

"Hell, we got money," Arthur told him, grinning.
"We'll buy another borrle." And to me, "Don't I say,
pal?"

"Naturally."

"Then I'll have the last one from the borrle."

He poured the red so that it fell into the glass with a
small tinkling sound, and it was dark and red and trans-
lucent in the electric light.

"Nothing like the red," Arthur said. "Jeripico. White
wine is awright, too, but nothing can beat the red." He
smiled at the boy and then winked at me. "He comes to
see the girl. The little one with the curls." And the boy
blushed, his face growing deep pink, his eyes turning
down in embarrassment.

"Leave him alone." I grinned. "You see he's shy."

"Ja. A very shy boy. Do you like the girl, ou pal?"

The boy blushed deeper; he didn't say anything, but
looked away from us.

"Leave him alone," I said to Arthur.

"He likes the girl very much," Arthur said, a little
drunkenly.

"Leave him alone, man, and order the other bottle,"
I said, and winked at the boy.

Arthur smiled at the boy, and then, turning to the door
to the back of the house, called, "Ma. Another borrle of
red. Asseblief. Please. Another one of the red."

"I heard you," the woman's voice growled from the
back. "Do you think I'm deaf?"

"No," Arthur replied. "Who said you was deaf? But
send another red, man. And let the girl bring it. The
lighty here is anxious to see her. He is a awake boy, a
real smart juba, and I like him."

"Lord God," Ma Schrikker's voice called again. "If
that is the case, make love to him. I would not put it past
you."

Arthur shook his head and looked lugubrious, saying
to me, "You see? Look at that now. Look at such
manners." He grinned at the boy again. "It's okay, pally.
Don't be afraid. I won't make love to you."

He laughed and slapped my shoulder, and after a while
Ma Schrikker herself came in. I saw the boy look up,
and saw the small disappointed look on his face.

"Where's Charlette?" I asked.

"She's gone to get the wine from the outhouse," Ma
said. "What, are you also courting her?"

"He does not like girls, what," Arthur said to her. He
laughed and went on: "My pally does not like girls.
There was a widow of forty-two who wanted to marry

him, but he turned her down due to lack of experience. His experience."

He laughed again and slapped my back once more, hiccoughing. "I ask excuse. Please excuse me." He tried to stand up and bow, but sat down again heavily.

"Gwarn," Ma Schrikker said. "You think you funny, mos."

"Charlie Chaplin," Arthur grinned.

Just then the girl came in carrying the bottle of red on a tray and Arthur said: "Hier's sy. Here she is. Your boy waits for you."

And looking at the girl, I saw the deep blush under her smooth, beautiful skin. Her skin was the color of amber wine, and she had dark brown eyes, bright and soft, and around her oval face her hair was very black and curly. The soft, full lips smiled shyly as she blushed. She did not look at the boy, but knew that he was there, and looking at him in turn I could see the deep flush of his own face and the gentle lowering of the eyelids as he watched her.

She placed the tray on the table and turned away. Arthur laughed. "No, man. Where can you go? With the boy here and all. Sit down, bokkie."

She blushed again and looked around the room, but not at the boy. I said, "Hullo, Charlette."

She glanced at me and blushed again and said "Hullo."

141

"Look how they blush," Arthur said teasingly. "Look how they blush, man."

He poured some of the red into his glass, his hand shaking a little, and passed the bottle to me. "They blush very nicely," he said, smiling.

"It's the love." Ma Schrikker laughed. She laughed so that her whole body shook. "Love. Just like in the bioscope."

Arthur lifted his glass in the direction of the boy and girl and announced, "To the bride and groom. May all your troubles be little ones."

He laughed again, and saw the hurt look in the boy's face, and the girl looking away. I was going to say something but Arthur interrupted. "With such love, blushing and all, these two must mos marry." He drank some of the wine, choked, and wiped his mouth on the back of his hand.

"Stop it," the girl said, and the boy looked across at Arthur.

"Stop watter?" Arthur asked blankly. "Stop the wedding? There must be a wedding." He got up as if he was going to propose a toast, but sat down again when his legs wouldn't hold him.

"Hell, cut it out, man," I told him. "Let's make finish and blow."

He looked puzzled. "What the hell, man. What goes on?"

The girl said, "Leave him alone. He's all right."

"Sure, I'm awright," Arthur said. "I can stand on one leg. You want to see?"

"You'll fall over and smash the furniture. All Ma's nice vases."

"Yes," Ma told him. "You watch my vases. They's presents I got. All of them."

"Bull," Arthur scowled, becoming lugubrious again. "Let's have another glass of wine, man."

I poured out two more glasses and took one. I smiled at the boy and said, "Don't worry about him. He's just had a few too many."

"That's okay," he answered, smiling. He looked at the girl and put one hand on her arm, gently, and she looked at him quickly, smiling with the small, curved smile. But there was something wrong, now, and a feeling of things not being the same.

Arthur finished his drink and hiccoughed again, saying sullenly, "To hell with it. I reckon they should get married. The next thing you'll know she'll have a belly, if you don't let them."

There was that look on the boy's face again and the girl, Charlette, got up and said angrily, "Stop it. How come you don't want to stop it?" She looked as if she wanted to cry, and Arthur got up, managing it this time, looking surprised.

143

"What'd I do?" he asked. "Now what did I do, man?"
He swayed on his feet.

I put a hand under his arm. "I reckon we better blow,"
I said.

"Ja," Ma Schrikker said. "He had enough. You better
take him home."

"Hell, I isn't drunk," Arthur said. "Let me go, man."

"No, man, you better go," Ma Schrikker told him.

"You throwing me out?" Arthur asked, looking at
her. "Awright." He looked at me and then at Ma again.
"You've lost a customer." And added haughtily, "A
good one, mos." He looked comical, all right, but I
didn't laugh.

I got him over to the door, with Ma following. Before
we went out I said to the girl and the boy, "Don't let
him upset you. He just had a few too many."

"It's all right," the girl said, not looking at me.

We went out onto the stoep and Arthur was sagging
on me a little. Ma said, standing in the doorway, looking
big and shapeless with the light behind her: "Now you
take him right home, hey? And don't get tackled."

"I'll get him home. He isn't very drunk."

"Let me go, man," Arthur said. "You reckon to carry
me. I can walk, man."

I said good-night to Ma and she said to come around
again, and shut the door on us.

"You awright?" I asked Arthur.

"Sure, man. Why not?"

"Let's go then."

"What the hell," he complained. "What they get so funny about?"

"You and your wedding," I told him as we went up the street. "You know that white boy can't marry the girl, even though he may love her. It isn't allowed."

"Jesus," Arthur said in the dark. "Jesus. What the hell."

THE PARTY

by James Matthews

THE ROOM WAS a large one, larger than any of the rooms in the houses he had been in previously. He scaled it mentally, comparing it with his own home. The two tiny bedrooms and the dining-living room would take up half of this comfortable room, leaving space for the kitchen and small yard. One end wall was covered with a tapestry and paintings, and gilt-framed mirrors covered the other walls. In one corner he nearly knocked an ivory carving from its pedestal. The carpet underneath his feet was as soft and lush as a municipal lawn.

Large as the room was, it could not contain the many people crowding it, and they spilled into the passage leading to the other rooms that led off it.

He gave what he hoped was a polite smile as the

147

woman squeezed into the small space left on the couch. He could feel her thigh pressing warm against his own. He wanted to edge his leg away but that would be too obvious, so he shifted his haunches to raise himself. She turned to him and smiled.

"Don't get up, please. I know it's a bit of a jam, but we should be able to manage."

He shifted his body so that she would have a little more space. "It's my fault," he said, "I'm taking up too much room."

"It's kind of you to say that, but I'm afraid it's my fault, really." She smiled as she patted her hip.

He nodded his head as if to assure her that he also had his troubles with a body that was not always what he would like it to be, and to show that he sympathized with her.

"Quite a crowd," she said.

"Yes," he replied.

"I wonder what has happened to the drinks? Have you been served?"

"No."

"Hold on to my seat and I'll see what I can do about it."

She was soon lost in the throng of bodies.

He changed his position so that his back rested against the angle formed by the arm of the couch and spread his legs so they covered the area between his neighbor and himself.

He looked at the many people in the room. There were a lot of women, outnumbering the men, and they were all white. Of the men, there were only four who were not white—himself and three others. The other three he knew well. Of the whites, he knew not one.

He was a stranger amongst strangers, and although they spoke the same tongue, because of his color he felt that he was deserted in a strange land.

He gazed around the room for his three friends and the assurance they would give him.

He spotted one, before the swelling line of bodies engulfed him. He had brief glimpses of another. Then a tightly packed group at the far end of the room attracted his attention. They parted to make way for a line of loudly talking, gesticulating women who wiggled their way across the room like a line of conga dancers on a cinema screen. He saw Ron before the group reformed, glass in one hand, the other poking into the air, emphasizing a point, self-assured. Then the gap was closed and he could only see backs.

He did not know what caused their interest, but whatever it was, Ron would dominate the conversation.

He envied Ron his calm, cool manner, his ability to mix without restraining thoughts about color, to bridge the gap as if there was none at all— or if there were a gap, then it did not apply to him.

His envy was without malice, and he hoped that with the passing of time he would also acquire that smoothness of manner and be forever rid of the uneasiness he felt now.

The room was loud with talk, but he could not separate the individual voices. The gruffer tones of the men merged with the shriller notes of the women, and, above the roar, like clanging cymbals, he could hear their laughter.

Snatches of conversation came to him like so many broadcasts from different stations, their only link the degree of noise.

"Jack has done it again!" The announcement was greeted with laughter. "By now one would think that he would have more sense."

He wondered who Jack was and what he had done to cause the speaker's concern and the mirth of his listeners.

"Are you going to Margo on Friday evening?"

"Yes, darling."

"Who will she have on show this time?"

"God alone knows! But if one is to judge by her previous dinners, it will be another genius of whose talent only Margo is aware. Are you going?"

"No, thanks, I'm not so hard up for a meal."

His misgivings returned. Was this what he was up against? How could he deal with them? In this jungle of polished manners and sharp tongues he would be defenseless—a black sacrificial lamb.

Ron had insisted that he go with them. The party was to celebrate the publication of a book, the author's third. Critics thought it important. When the first book was

published, he had become a supporter of the author, reading everything he wrote. When told by Ron that a meeting could be arranged he had at first backed out, but the
invitation, or rather, Ron, changed his mind.

"Look, William. I went to all the trouble to get you an
invitation to the party so that you can meet Colin Ashworth. It's about time you start meeting people and going
places," Ron had said.

He flushed when he thought of the meeting fifteen
minutes earlier.

"Colin. This is William Apollis. He swears by you as a
writer," Ron said, introducing him. He stiffly poked out a
hand to meet that of a white man a head taller than himself. "How do you do?" he said, hating himself for uttering the conventional inanity.

"So this is the William you've told me about." Turning
to him, the white man continued: "I hear you also write,
William. Would you let me have a look at some of your
stuff, soon?"

He looked into a pair of understanding eyes. A choking
heat filled him. "Yes . . . yes," he stammered.

"Excuse me for a moment." Their host left them to
greet a couple entering.

As they crossed the room, Ron called greetings to
several people, stopping to speak to some of them before
passing on. During their progress William got separated
from the others and made for the couch.

A tray was held before him, and as he reached for a

glass filled with sherry, he caught a glimpse of a bare bosom. He could not stop himself looking at the breasts so temptingly displayed. The woman moved toward the next person, unaware of the havoc aroused within him.

He looked at the women in their form-fitting dresses with low necklines, and again he had the feeling that they should have been on the cinema screen. From where he sat their movements gave him a three-dimensional effect, their chatter providing the script for the scene.

Immersed in the idea, he forgot the people seated next to him and concentrated on the changing pattern. His eyes focused on a particular person, lost him, then found him again. A woman attracted him. She was not young, but she had a bearing that compensated for her lost youth. She could only play the part of a queen or a duchess. The game delighted him and he followed it in earnest, counting how many times he could pick her out before finally losing her.

He was aware that someone was looking at him, and guiltily raised his head, like a little boy caught peeping at forbidden things.

It was the woman who had offered to get him a drink.

She had a tray on which was balanced a plate filled with snacks, a bowl of mixed nuts, and two glasses of gin and lime.

He jumped to his feet.

"Please, sit down," she said after seating herself, shifting her body so that he could fit in.

He sank down beside her.

"I've brought something to nibble at. I don't think you've had anything to eat since you came. I see you have a drink at least. Oh, well! You can have this one, too."

"No, thank you."

"Do have it," she urged him. "Besides, I have been here longer than you."

He took the second drink, carefully placing his empty glass at the side of the tray.

"What do you do?"

The friendliness of her smile soothed his caution.

"I write," he said, "at least, I try."

"Have you had anything published?"

"Five." Then he stopped, dismayed at his school-boy eagerness.

"Where were they published?" she prompted him.

"They were all published locally, except for one—'The Flower Seller'—which was published in London."

"Wait a minute! I think I've read it. Yes, I have. It was in *Argosy*, wasn't it? I loved it. So you are William Apollis." A glow of warmth swept over him at her remembering the name of the writer. "You also wrote 'The Char's Birthday Wish' and 'The Golden Penny.' I always thought that those stories were not written by white writers. They were too authentic, too close to the subject." She touched him lightly on the shoulder. "You know what I mean. I must say it's a pleasure meeting you after enjoying your stories so much."

She held out her hand. "I'm Margo Pearce." He

gingerly wrapped his hand around her soft one. He wondered whether she was the same Margo who invited the dullest people to her dinners. As if to confirm it, she said, "You must come to dinner and a drink at my place. Then we can really have a talk. There are some people I would like you to meet." She mentioned a few names—writers, artists, a sculptor—people Ron had told him about. Not too well-known names, but all considered as going to make their mark.

He burst out laughing. He could not help himself as he thought of the two women and their conversation. How wrong both of them must be! If the people mentioned were dull, then the company those two moved in must be the wittiest and most talented in the land.

She looked at him, puzzled. "Is it so funny, my asking you to dinner?"

"No, it's not that. I just thought of something someone had said." All the time he was telling himself that it had a funny side. Dinner in a big house. He imagined how it would be, at a long table covered with a stiffly starched white cloth on which would be placed an array of knives and forks. At home, his mother always served dinner in the kitchen. The only time they ate in the dining room was on religious holidays.

"When would you be able to come? Would next Friday do? I could arrange for someone to pick you up, or if you prefer, you could come out by bus. I'm at 3 Anchor Bay,

St. John's Road. You can't miss it. It's a small house with a block of flats on each side."

He searched for an excuse.

There was a difference between a party like this and a dinner, he reasoned. Here there was the safety of numbers. He could withdraw into himself and be lost in the shuffle, but a dinner party would be more intimate. Would he know the right thing to do? What if he should choose the wrong spoon or fork? Would they laugh at the blunder or would they ignore it and try to cover it with their talk? Both ways would be painful to him. It would be better to refuse.

He was undecided. He very much wanted to be in the presence of the people she had mentioned; he felt the need to mix with those who had the same yearning as himself. From across the room Ron waved at him before being swept up into another group. He felt reassured. He would go.

"It would be less bother if I come out by bus."

"It's no bother, William."

"I'm sure I would be able to find the place on my own, ma'am."

"I shall be very angry if you don't call me Margo. Everyone else does."

He rolled her name on his tongue a few times, savoring it before uttering: "Margo."

"Margo, dear. I don't think I have been introduced to your friend."

He looked at a tall, slender young man, a study in black and white. His dark hair, brushed flat on the skull, contrasted sharply with his pale face. His eyes matched his hair, and above them his eyebrows were two streaks of black. He was dressed in a black suit, with white shirt and pencil-slim black tie.

"Oh. It's you, Edward. Meet William Apollis. He's going to be a first-rate writer. Remember, I'm the one who told you." She turned toward him. "William, this is Edward Blakely."

Both name and face were familiar. Then he recalled. Blakely was a member of the Liberal Party or Congress of Democrats, he was not sure which.

Again he felt that awkwardness when he shook hands.

"William is coming to dinner next Friday. You are still coming, aren't you?"

"Of course, Margo." Then to William, "Would you excuse us for a moment? There are some people who want to meet Margo."

"Not at all." He felt bold enough to add, "Then I'll see you next Friday, Margo?"

"Yes, and do bring along some of your work."

Then they were absorbed by the crowd.

He leaned back, breathing deeply. The bustling scene —was he to be a part of it? Would he be able to fit in freely without the constant inner fear that perhaps he did not belong?

The thought that had plagued him returned.

Would she have asked him to dinner if he were not the writer of the stories she had enjoyed so much? What would her reactions have been if he had told her otherwise? That he was as nondescript as he looked, that he came mainly through Ron's urgings?

The doubt awoke other thoughts he had tried to bury.

These people, Ron had said, made no fuss about the color of one's skin, accepted one for what one was, but were they really so open and casual or was it a pose they all assumed?

"Do you intend sitting on this couch for the rest of the evening?" Ron stood in front of him. "What has happened to Margo? I saw her speaking to you a little while ago."

"She left with another chap, Edward Blakely, who said that there were some people who wanted to meet her."

"Oh, Edward. Looking like a corpse as usual with his pale face and black eyes. What do you think of Margo?"

"She seems to be quite nice. She has—"

"Yes, I know. She has invited you to dinner. She fancies herself a patron of the arts. She should have lived in the eighteenth century—then she could have turned her home into a salon. At least you're making progress. It's about time that you crawled out of your shell. It's at parties like this that you'll meet people, important people who can really help you a lot if you go about it in the right way."

He made no reply, silently wondering what the right way was.

Recalling Ron's attitude nine months before, he was not sure whether he should be grateful now. He had had his first story published. Previously Ron had scarcely spoken a dozen words to him, including him among those tolerated but never asked to meet the white friends of whom Ron spoke so intimately and whose names were often featured on the social page of the local newspapers. The few times Ron had spoken to him, he had repeatedly pointed out William's lack of feeling for art in any form.

His story had brought a change.

"I've read your story," Ron had said. "It's not a bad effort. Is it your first?"

"No, it's not," he replied. "I've written several but it's the first one published."

"Why all the secrecy? Why didn't you tell me you were interested in creative writing? There are some chaps I could have introduced you to. Established writers."

A second and third story published made him a member of the select few Ron favored.

"Come along with us tomorrow evening. Tom Hopkirk is having a party at his place in Devil's Peak."

"No," he had replied.

During the months that passed, Ron often urged him to accompany them, but always his answer was, "No!" The picture of himself mixing socially with whites filled him with dread. The whites at work smiled at him and spoke to him, then forgot him, remembering him only when they wanted something done. The more Ron spoke of the parties he had been to and the people he met, the less became his resistance and the stronger the yearning to meet and become part of the groups Ron described. When Ron told him about the invitation from Colin Ashworth, he could not hold out any longer and accepted.

"Let's join the others," Ron said now.

"No. I'll sit here a little while longer. Perhaps Margo will come back and we can continue our talk."

He was pathetically grateful for the friendliness of Margo and the understanding shown by Colin Ashworth.

Ron looked at him with raised eyebrows, then left him.

Another woman sank down beside him. It was the woman he had dubbed "duchess."

She gazed at him as if he were a curio. She should have had a lorgnette, he thought. Then she spoke. "Tell me, what do you do?" Her voice was cold and condescending.

Her tone and manner chilled him, and he felt an instant dislike.

"Do?"

"Yes!"

"I work in an office. I'm a"—he thought of saying clerk—"I'm a messenger."

"I don't mean your type of work." Waving it aside as if it was a distasteful object. "Do you paint or write? If I like what you do, I can be very helpful."

"No."

"Come now. I bet that isn't true. The others do either one or the other."

There was no need to ask who the others were, and she must obviously be one of the important people Ron had told him about.

"I've told you the truth. I don't do a thing."

He was not worried about deceiving her. If she were to check with Ron it would be just too bad. She was not going to add him to her collection.

"You don't paint and you don't write and you are a messenger?" Her eyes and voice jabbed at him.

"That's right."

"Then what are you doing here?" she shot at him.

"The same thing you are doing." His dislike for her strengthened him, overcoming his trembling. "I'm here because I was invited."

"I don't want any of your damn cheek!" Her voice jumped several octaves.

People seated on the couch and those nearby turned to stare.

She got up, nostrils flaring and breath drawn in audible snorts.

A horrified Ron pushed his way toward them.

"Mrs. Meredith, what is the matter?" he exclaimed. "What has happened?"

"I have been insulted by this impertinent messenger boy!" she said, pointing an accusing finger at William.

Ron faced him. "Get up and apologize at once!" he said, his voice thick with reproach.

William looked at Ron, whose composure was crumbling with the effort to placate Mrs. Meredith. He was sick to the stomach at what he considered a betrayal on Ron's part, and his former unease gave way to anger.

She would have accepted him if he had told her that he too was a writer, and here was Ron, without hearing his side of it, taking her part.

His admiration for Ron turned to contempt. He knew why Ron had been so ingratiating. His talents, and those of the others, were on display like virgins to be sold to those like her, and Ron was their pimp.

It was for this, to walk in the shadow of a Mrs. Meredith, that Ron had snubbed the others, pushed them aside, forgetting that he too came from them. And this was what he had envied him for. The ability to converse and move with ease among them, to provide another virgin for their inspection. His anger brought a flood of blood to his head, making speech impossible as he glared at Ron. He got up from the couch and blindly pushed his way through the animated throng, not aware of the approval evident in Margo Pearce's eyes.

The Outsider

*The endurance of the inequalities of
life is the marvel of human society.*
—JAMES FROUDE

NOCTURNE

by Alex La Guma

꧁꧂꧁꧂꧁꧂꧁꧂꧁꧂꧁꧂꧁꧂꧁꧂

THERE WERE THREE of them sitting at the table near
the window. At that time of the afternoon the Duke's
Head was quiet. The plump barman wiped the smooth,
stained teak in front of him. At the end of the bar a
haggard man sat like a lone penitent in a cathedral and
slowly sipped his flat beer. Somewhere across the street
somebody was playing a piano. The three at the table were
drinking beer and port and talking quietly.

"It's easy," Moos was saying. "Frog will be outside
holding candle. You and I, Harry, will get in and floor
the watchman. Hell, Harry, you aren't listening."

Harry was listening to the piano across the street. The
music came through the open window, now tinkling like
water dripping into a fine china bowl, now throbbing

and booming with the sound of many beautiful tuned gongs, rippling away and rising again in great waves.

"God, what playing," Harry said, as the piece ebbed to a gentle finish. "Did you rookers hear that?"

"——," Moos said. "Classical stuff. Just a helluva noise. Give me a wakker jol any time." He dismissed the subject by taking a swallow of beer. "Now listen. We'll go over it again . . ."

"I know, I know," Harry said. "Frog is outside keeping watch. We'll be inside fixing the watchman. Now, what time do we meet?"

"Nine," Moos answered. "I'll pick Frog up and we'll get you outside the Modern."

"How much you think we'll pick up?" Frog asked, drinking some of his port. The piano started again, the music drifting cautiously into the barroom.

"About a hundred and forty or fifty," Moos said. He was aware of the sound again, but ignored it. Only Harry continued to listen. He sipped his port and let his mind lap at the music. The gentle, perfect notes touched something inside him, and he got a strange feeling, but did not try to fathom it. He kept listening. He tried the air under his breath, struggling with it like a terrier with an expensive slipper, and gave it up to listen again. The piano music quivered and undulated. Once a car passed and drowned it momentarily, but it emerged again, gentle as the drop of tears. It was the *Nocturne No. 2*, in E flat major, by Chopin, but Harry did not know that.

Moos and Frog began talking about other things as the piano drifted into the *Fantasie-Impromptu*. Harry was completely absorbed in the music now. It held him in its spell, tying him to itself with wires of throbbing sound, drugging his mind into a coma of swelling and fading rhythm. The music went on, seemingly inexhaustible: Liszt's *Hungarian Rhapsody* pounded and crashed, the theme from Tchaikowsky's *Pathétique* wept quietly, waltzes and minuets pranced and cavorted, pieces of Beethoven marched somberly, and Spanish gypsy dances whirled and stamped. Schubert's *Serenade* called longingly to some unknown lover in a darkened room. The *Nocturne* came again, drifting with the step of fairies on moonlit grass.

The Duke's Head began to fill up steadily with the six o'clock crowd, until the music was lost in the steady hum of voices. Harry got up and wandered to the bar. The spell was broken. He whistled softly through his teeth, trying to capture a tune, but his mind had not drunk deeply enough of the music. He joined the three-deep line at the bar and shouldered his way through until he could order half-a-pint of white wine. He leaned against the wet teakwood and drank quietly, still trying to remember. Around him men discussed every topic imaginable: work, races, politics, women, wine, bioscope, religion. A dirty and disheveled man came in, selling pickles and curry pies. At one end of the bar an argument developed, and for a few moments there was uproar, until the plump barman broke it up.

Somebody tapped Harry on the shoulder and he turned his head. It was Moos.

"Nine o'clock. Don't forget."

"Okay. Okay. See you later."

Harry did not watch Moos and Frog go out. He finished the white wine and then extricated himself from the jam at the bar and pushed past the swinging doors into the street. He paused on the pavement. It was growing dark, and the street lamps were on. From diagonally across the way the piano music was still going on, a little louder now that he was outside. It came from an old two-story building, one of a row that formed one side of the grimy street.

He stood for a while and listened, and then strolled down the pavement, looking across at the house, drawn by the music like an alley cat drawn by the scent of fresh and tender meat.

Drab and haunted-looking people sat in doorways looking like scarred saints among the ruins of abandoned churches, half listening, gossiping idly, while the pinched children shot at each other with wooden guns from behind overflowing dustbins in the dusk. Harry crossed the street and paused, hesitating, outside the house.

The music gripped him again. It came from a half-open window on the first floor, bubbling out like a spring of cool water in a wasteland. Then he made up his mind suddenly and climbed the chipped front steps and edged into the house. The hallway was dim and smelled of stale cooking and carbolic water. The sound came from the upper landing, slipping down the worn staircase, echoing from the gloomy corners and the high, stained ceiling. He climbed the stairs slowly, advancing into the crescendo of Ravel's *Bolero*.

Outside the door he stopped, nervous now, a little afraid, but soaked in the music. He stood there while the *Bolero* ended in its crashing chords. Sound came again, tirelessly, gently, moonbeam quivering on quiet waters, on trees and grass along a lonely river bank, sighing for love, and he placed his hand on the doorknob and turned it.

The music faded away like a cataract in a little mountain nook quietly running dry, and the girl at the piano looked at him with sudden surprise.

"I'm sorry if I scared you," he said, holding the door open. "I've been listening to you playing from across the way. Real good music."

"Thank you. Do you like it?"

"Don't know anything about it. But it sounds pretty."

"Come in and sit down if you want to," she said. "People around here often come in to listen."

"Thanks, miss."

He entered, awkward as a tramp being admitted to a parish tea, and was suddenly conscious of the port-wine smell on his breath. He sat down on a straight chair as if he expected it to collapse under his weight. The room was neat, dustless, polished, the little tables cluttered with bric-a-brac, framed music-school certificates hanging with Queen Victoria, wedding groups, and *God Is Love* along the papered walls. Another door led to an adjoining room. The whole place seemed to struggle for survival with the surrounding dilapidation, like a Siamese cat caught in a sewer.

"You learn to play by yourself?" he asked, scarcely daring to speak aloud.

"Oh, no. I studied in a convent."

"What's it bring you? It's pretty, but what's it bring you? Money?"

"Money's not everything. People come up here to listen." She smiled at him and ran her fingers along the keys. Her face was dark and fine and delicate as a costly violin."What do you want me to play?"

Harry cleared his throat and said: "That piece you were playing when I came in. It sounded good."

"The *Moonlight Sonata*." And the music welled up again, falling on him like a gentle rain. He sat straight up, listening, and his muscles relaxed and his mind forgot the nervousness and he sank back in the chair.

"I never had a chance to listen to this kind of stuff," he said, when it had ended. "High bugs go to the City Hall to hear it." He wiped his mouth on the back of his hand and went on: "There's another piece I heard you play. Goes like this." He pursed his lips and struggled with the tune and managed a few notes while she listened. He tried again and managed a few jumbled bars this time. Then he gave it up, shaking his head and grinning shyly.

But she had caught it and her hands moved again, gentle as the fall of a hair, and the music poured from her fingertips. "You mean Chopin's *Nocturne*."

"Is that what it's called? Yes, that's it."

He leaned back and shut his eyes and whistled soundlessly with the music, taking it in completely. She played it twice and his head nodded in time.

After that the old-fashioned clock on the sideboard caught his eye and he remembered with a little start that Moos and Frog would be waiting for him. He got up quickly and said: "I won't keep you any longer. I've got to be going, anyhow."

"Did you enjoy it?"

"Really. I'd like to come again, some other time."

"Of course. Come any evening."

"Thanks, miss. Well, good luck."

"Good-by. Thanks for coming in to listen."

He was out in the dark street again and hurried up it. The doorstep sitters had withdrawn now and the windows of the tenements were yellow with lamplight. Babies wailed here and there, hangers-on lounged against walls, couples made furtive love in doorways. Somewhere beyond, neon signs made a glare against the sky, like a city after a bombardment.

Moos and Frog were waiting impatiently in the light of a shopfront, smoking and cursing fretfully.

171

"Where the——you been?" Moos asked angrily. "We been waiting."

"Awright, awright. I'm here now," Harry said. "Let's go."

They walked down the street together. Harry was still thinking about the girl who played the piano, and that he didn't even know her name. He whistled quietly. Knock something, she had said it was. Funny name. He thought, sentimentally, that it would be real smart to have a goose that played the piano like that.

DEBUT

by Alf Wannenburgh

IT WAS ONLY after he had searched the back streets of Cape Town for half an hour that Paul found Governor's Lane. He counted the houses from the corner and parked his car.

Somewhere inside the semidetached cottage a recorded saxophone wailed its plaintive appeal. He climbed the three steps from the pavement and knocked cautiously on the front door. Then he moved slightly to one side, so that the first light from the opened door would not fall directly on him, and stood, whistling softly to himself, allowing his eyes to wander over the jungle of potted ferns on the stoep. Deep in his stomach he could feel the fortifying warmth of the brandy he had drunk in preparation for the party. There was no answer to his knock. Inside, the saxophone continued to plead.

He knocked again, this time more boldly, and glanced

at his watch. It was eight o'clock. Right on time, he thought. A brief, late visit could so easily be interpreted as that of a self-opinionated junior clerk who condescends to accept a messenger's invitation to his sister's engagement party. Well, arriving early like this should prove to Lionel that he came because he really wanted to spend the evening with them, and that he was not merely dropping in out of curiosity, or as a matter of form. Slumming.

What Paul feared most was that his motives would be misunderstood. Originally, he had pressed Lionel for an invitation because he wanted to penetrate the official status-barrier between them, and he had been confident that his request would be regarded as sincere. But as the time between the invitation and the party had shortened, his confidence had diminished. "Are you quite sure it's all right?" he had asked on a number of occasions. And each time Lionel would stare blankly at him for a moment and then hasten, in his servile fashion, to assure him that it really was so. He wasn't sure whether Lionel's expression *was* blank, or dead pan. What did he think? What did he feel? Now he was thankful for the brandy's added reassurance.

As he raised his hand to knock a third time, the door opened about three inches and a small, brown face looked up at him. Looked up at him, and said nothing.

"Is Lionel Petersen home?" he asked, after a moment of mutually uncertain silence.

The child continued to stare up at him. She did not reply.

"Does Lionel Petersen live here?"

He stepped into the light. Without moving her body, the child swept him with her eyes, as if she was trying to divine his reason for being there from his appearance.

"Please, I'm looking for Lionel Petersen!"

The child turned her face from the opening and shouted: "Lionel, there's a white man here by the door to see you."

The door opened a few inches further to reveal an apple-green, linoleum-covered entrance hall. There were no signs of a party. Not the slightest indication. But surely Lionel had confirmed it only the previous afternoon. Paul couldn't possibly have made the mistake of coming on the wrong night?

"Lionel! A white man!"

Paul winced. There was no answer from inside and the small, brown face disappeared. The door closed, leaving the stoep in darkness. He altered the position of his feet indecisively and fumbled for his cigarettes. The saxophone wept tremulously into a blues passage.

Then suddenly the door swung wide open. "I'm terribly sorry for keeping you waiting like this, sir, but I wasn't expecting you to come so early."

"That's quite all right, Lionel. I was just beginning to wonder whether I had come to the right house."

"Oh, yes, sir."

Paul was ushered into a small pink sitting room. The carpet had been rolled up along one wall in anticipation of dancing, and the room was empty of furniture, save for a highly-polished gram-radio and a pair of easy chairs in which sprawled two youths, wearing blue jeans and pictured shirts, who were reading vividly colored American comics. They turned their eyes toward him and nodded. Lionel did not introduce them. Self-consciously, they gathered their scattered comics from the floor and left the room.

Lionel turned down the volume of the record player. "My younger brothers," he said, jerking his head in the direction of the doorway.

"I see—but there was really no need for them to go out."

"They have to go and change, anyway, sir."

Lionel began smoothing the upholstery of one of the easy chairs. "If you will just make yourself comfortable, sir." He patted the cushion back into shape. "You see, sir, no one else has arrived yet. My sister and her friends have gone to an early show at the Gem. They should be back in about half an hour. I've just been helping with things in the kitchen."

"Please don't let me get in your way."

"Not at all, sir."

"Another thing, Lionel—" Paul felt decidedly ill at ease. He had known before he came that he would have to say this, and had carefully rehearsed his words; but

176

now he felt that he was only erecting another barrier by repeating them. "My name tonight is Paul. Please don't call me anything else in front of your friends. I want to be treated exactly like your other guests. Please."

"Yes, sir."

"Yes . . .?"

"It's not easy for me to change my whole way of thinking just like that, sir."

Paul shrugged. He could feel the color rising in his cheeks. This was not as he had wanted it to be. It was all so damn formal. He had expected to arrive in the middle of the party, when all the stiffness of their workday relationship would be dissolved in a exciting swirl of enjoyment. Instead, they were alone together. Alone, with the wedge of rank thrusting itself between them. "Please try," he said.

"Can I get you a drink, sir?"

"Thank you, yes."

"Something in particular?"

"I'll have some—What is it you colored people usually drink?" He vaguely recalled some smug office joke, and remembered bottle store window displays he had seen. "Oh, yes, I'll have some of that wine. Oom Tas, isn't it?"

"I can give you anything you like, sir. Brandy, gin, vodka?"

"No. No. I want to be like everybody else. Just give me a glass of Oom Tas, please."

Lionel stiffened. "I'm sorry, but we never keep any Oom Tas, sir. If you want wine, I can get you some sherry."

Paul noticed the curl of distaste that came to his lips and the note of restrained contempt in the way he said "Oom Tas," and he felt that Lionel was being, deliberately, very patient with him, as if he were teaching him a lesson. Paul hoped that he had not said anything which had offended him.

"Make it brandy then."

While Lionel went to fetch him a drink from another room, Paul sat and looked at the framed Tretchikoff print and illuminated text, *God is Head of This House,* which faced each other from opposing walls. Damn it, why couldn't he relax?

Faint female laughter rippled nervously in the entrance hall and Lionel returned with a bottle and glass. He was followed, hesitantly, by a plump woman whose white apron accentuated the bulbous prominence of the maternal breasts that pressed against the restraining floral fabric of her dress.

"Mr. Anderson, this is my mother."

"Very pleased to meet you, Mrs. Petersen."

She bobbed her head and gave him a toothless smile. For a moment no one said anything and she began shyly backing toward the door. "I'm very glad you were able to come," she managed. "Lionel often speaks about you."

"Thank you." And then, turning to Lionel as Mrs.

Petersen slipped from view, Paul said: "I'm sorry if I said anything that offended you."

"That's quite all right, sir."

"I also find it difficult to change my whole way of thinking, you know."

"I understand, sir."

Lionel poured some brandy into the glass and handed it to him. Paul felt the warm flush of his embarrassment meet and mingle with the already present glow of the brandy in his stomach. Just a few more should loosen him up nicely. He took the glass and drank deeply, feeling the raw flame of the spirits blazing through his throat and chest. That was much better. Already he could feel the difference.

"Thanks. Just what I needed."

Lionel refilled his glass.

"I think we're beginning to understand each other, don't you?"

"Yes, sir," Lionel repeated dutifully.

There was a knock at the front door. A youth of about twenty, wearing a carefully pressed, diamond-black suit and silver tie, was admitted to the room. He glanced apologetically from one to the other, nodded timidly, slunk across to the vacant chair opposite Paul and sat down. He did not raise his eyes, and apparently he expected to be ignored.

"Would you introduce us?" Paul said to Lionel.

Immediately the youth looked up and gave him an ingratiating smile.

"I'm sorry, sir. Tony Williams, this is Mr. Anderson— from the office where I work."

Paul clasped the extended hand firmly, and felt it crumple. It was damp and boneless, and he dropped it as soon as he felt its texture. Tony Williams continued to smile.

"Lionel!" a voice called from somewhere at the back of the house. Lionel excused himself. Tony Williams and Paul glanced uncertainly at each other.

"You're not at the cinema with the others?" said Paul.

"No, Mr. Anderson," Tony Williams responded eagerly. "You see, they only told me they were going after they had booked their seats already." He seemed relieved and grateful to Paul for having spoken to him.

"You a close friend of Lionel and his sister?"

"No, our mothers are friends."

"I see." Paul lapsed into silence, searching for a new topic with which to continue the conversation. He felt unpleasantly drowsy, and he knew if he closed his eyes he would experience a languid, floating sensation. Brandy always affected him that way.

"Cigarette, Mr. Anderson?" Tony Williams flashed an ornate cigarette case in front of Paul. "Solid silver," he said, proudly tapping the lid. "Belonged to my grandfather."

"Very nice."

"He was a European, like you."

"I beg your pardon?"

"I said my grandfather was white. He was Irish. I'm mostly white myself, though you wouldn't say so to look at me. Would you?"

Paul looked at the dark-skinned youth and was quite certain that he would not. "I don't know," he said.

"Well, I am. Well, almost—my grandfather came from Ireland."

Paul found the conversation embarrassing. He disliked the way Tony Williams claimed his white ancestry. "It doesn't matter to me, really."

"You see, a lot of colored people have native blood," Tony Williams continued. "You can tell by their hair. Now there's nothing like that in my family."

Paul wished that the conversation would end. "I don't see that it's important."

"But it is, Mr. Anderson, because those who haven't got straight hair are mostly the skollies. Those with native hair. That's why I'm glad when a European gentleman like you comes to one of our parties, because then you can see that some of us are respectable, and that all colored people aren't like that. You know, sometimes I feel ashamed that I'm colored. But as I told you about my grandfather . . ."

Paul was swept by a sudden feeling of revulsion. Why? Why did they have to keep reminding him that he was different? "A European gentleman." Did they think he had come to censor their enjoyment? To confirm or discard a previously held prejudice? All he wanted was to belong, to be accepted simply as another guest at the party. Just another guest.

"Is something wrong, Mr. Anderson?" Tony Williams was leaning forward with exaggerated concern. "Another drink?"

Paul held out his glass. Outside there were sounds of laughter, and a moment later a crowd of young people swarmed into the room. They hesitated briefly when they saw Paul and Tony Williams, and their exuberance dissolved. A few of them nodded indefinitely at Paul, the remainder ignored him—not deliberately, as a slight, but rather as if they had been caught in an unfamiliar situation, and not knowing what they should do, did nothing. Tony Williams was pointedly ignored. He lowered his eyes and seemed to shrink into his chair. He made no attempt to greet them.

After the first shock of finding a stranger in the room, their chatter revived quickly. The men made their exit in a group and went toward the room that served as a bar, while the girls pressed around the record player, excitedly disagreeing about the title of the first tune they wanted to play.

Paul jumped to his feet and, with an extravagant display of chivalry, offered his chair to any of the ladies who might wish to sit. A few giggled. None accepted.

He was disconcerted by their reticence and wanted to escape. Women had a way of humiliating one with just the faintest suggestion of laughter. They were so adept at it.

"Come, shall we join the men in the bar?" he said to Tony Williams, who appeared indifferent as to whether he was ignored by the men or the women. He unwound from his chair, slowly and without enthusiasm, and followed Paul at a short distance.

The bar was crowded. A table had been placed across one corner of the room, and its top was covered by a brightly colored beach towel, on which were arranged rows of sparkling tumblers, a basin of water for rinsing them, and assorted bottles of liquor. When Paul paused in the doorway, the clamor for drinks terminated suddenly and the crowd parted to allow him immediate access to the table.

"Yes, sir. What can I do for you, sir?" asked the plump, red-faced man with rolled-up shirt sleeves who stood behind the table, his trousers suspended, beneath a protruding stomach, by a pair of broad black braces.

Paul flushed. "First come, first served," he said with strained casualness. "I'll wait my turn."

Lionel appeared beside him suddenly and touched him lightly on the arm. "Go ahead, sir, let him fill your glass. It's the first time we've had a European at one of our parties."

Paul wanted to protest but found himself being led

by Lionel through the parted crowd, which closed behind them as they passed, leaving Tony Williams alone at the door. He accepted the drink Lionel handed to him and then turned. "Please," he said to all who were in the room, his voice choking self-consciously, "don't treat me like a European. I have that all day at work. This is the first time I'm coming to one of your parties, and I want you to think of me as one of yourselves." He added a second "please." Then they parted again, and he returned through the crowd to the door.

"That was very good, Mr. Anderson," Tony Williams said, feeling for Paul's hand. "Most of these people don't deserve you treating them like they were equals. But it was very nice what you just said."

The crowd had closed again behind Paul. Backs were turned toward him. Drinks were being served and consumed.

"The only good white man is a dead one," said someone in the thick of the crowd, and everybody laughed, a trifle nervously, because perhaps that was going a little too far. Paul also laughed. He laughed louder than anyone else because he wanted them to know that he understood the quip in the spirit of a joke. He was still laughing when they had stopped. But when he stopped, they all started again. He handed his empty glass to Tony Williams and began searching for the bathroom, followed by the sounds of their amusement.

There he sat for a while, feeling the damp chill of the

cement floor seeping through the seat of his trousers, his forehead resting on the white enamel coolness of the rim of the bath. Once there was an urgent knocking at the bathroom door. Then he heard someone being directed to go outside, and after that he was not disturbed again.

When he had resolved the threatening conflict in his stomach, he stood up and placed his ear against the door. All sounds seemed to be coming from the front of the house. He inched the door open gingerly, and seeing that nobody was in the vicinity, with hands outstretched for support from the walls on both sides of the passage, he began feeling his way toward the room in which they were dancing.

Bright-eyed young people spun and writhed before him in a confusion of movement and color, while the older, more sedate couples glided effortlessly between the gyrating figures, lost in the somnambulent smoothness of their rhythm. Then, suddenly, it was not only the dancers who were moving; gray streaks like heavy rain shot across his vision, and the music receded into the background and was replaced by a monotonous, low humming in his ears. Then the whole room began to turn. Around, and around, and around and around; his head seemed to be revolving with rapidly increasing momentum through a narrowing tunnel of sound in ever tightening spirals—faster, faster, faster. Where to? He fought down the mounting pangs of nausea and pushed his head back hard against the wall, fixing his eyes on the illuminated text opposite him, *God is Head of This House.* It was as if he was standing in a constantly shaken kaleidoscope. And then, slowly, he gained control over his own internal movement, and he was able to separate the stationary objects from the dancers who continued to move, swaying and twisting.

As Paul watched, he noticed that some of the dancers glanced occasionally in his direction and then turned and whispered to their partners, who looked at him with furtive, suppressed smiles. But although these smiles were directed at him, they did not invite his participation. He inspected his clothing, but could find no possible cause for mirth. But then, they were not quite smiles of mirth. They were rather of the sort that set him apart—that isolated him. And as he watched, he longed to participate, to be accepted as one of them. Maybe they thought that he was holding himself aloof? Yes. That was it. He must show them that he was not aloof.

Slowly, he allowed his eyes to wander around the edge of the room, and he noticed that the only other person who seemed to be left outside the general excitement was a girl who was darker than the rest, and who had what Tony Williams had called "native" hair. Was that the reason why no one paid her any attention? Then he would dance with her. That would show them that he wasn't aloof.

He stumbled across the room and seized her hand. "Come. Let's dance," he shouted above the din.

"No," she said. "Please, I'm not feeling well."

But already he had pulled her out onto the floor, and they were caught in the vortex of swirling bodies.

"Please," she said again, more urgently.

He smiled abandonedly. "We'll show them," he said, flinging her out at arm's length and then suddenly jerking her back toward him. The brandy throbbed behind his temples. "Let's go!" His heels flashed up alternately behind him in a preposterous distortion of the Charleston. The other dancers edged away from them. His right heel caught the net apron of a satin dress. It hooked for a fraction of a second, and then he felt the materials part. There was a short, sharp scream of protest. "Sorry!" he shouted over his shoulder, and then his feet continued to work like flails, a piece of pink net flying from the heel of his shoe like a flag.

Then Paul and his dark partner were alone on the floor. The other dancers stood around the fringes of the room and waited for them to stop.

"Please!" his partner repeated, struggling.

"We'll show them! Don't be shy," he shouted, raising her arm to form an arch and ducking beneath it.

"Please!" she said again. And then her feet stopped moving. But he clung to her limp arm and pranced about her, calling encouragement. Then, as the music reached its climax, he grabbed her in his arms and spun her round and round in a final flourish that ended with a kiss on her cheek.

She turned her face away from him and tried to free her hands.

When the music stopped, the room continued to revolve against the direction in which he felt himself to be turning. He dropped the girl's arms, and leaving her standing alone in the center of the floor, he reeled toward the door. He had to get to the bathroom, quickly. Christ, he had to get to the bathroom. But the doorway and the passage were choked with laughing people, all of whom seemed to be clutching at his arms and coat sleeves. God, how they were laughing! Cluster upon cluster of laughing brown faces. Row upon row of laughing brown faces. God, how they were laughing! But he didn't mind their being brown. Anyone could have any damn color face he liked. Please, God, he had to get to the bathroom. Blue, pink, white, green, and even brown, what did he care, as long as he got to the bathroom. And then he was going to be nice to those brown faces. He liked them, and he was going to show them that he liked them. They would see. And still the faces were laughing—rows of white teeth like endless piano keyboards.

He staggered between them, pulling the tails of his unbuttoned jacket behind him, shrugging off the hands that grabbed at his shoulders, until he came at last to the bathroom door.

It was locked.

He rattled the handle and beat on the panels with the palms of his hands. It remained locked. Then he twisted around so that his shoulders were flat against the wall, slid slowly down to a sitting position on the apple-green linoleum beside the door, and placed his head between his knees.

The laughter came to him from the passage in terrifying waves of unreality.

God, he would show them!

He felt the saliva running thin in his mouth and his stomach heaved.

Then suddenly the laughing stopped.

Now Lionel and Tony Williams were beside him. "Just a moment and we'll make you comfortable, sir."

He was being lifted. "No. No. Jus' a faintin' spell. Wan' t' be like ever'body else . . ." He saw Mrs. Petersen shaking stiff white sheets out over the bed. And then he was alone in the dark room.

"Why these whites always got to show off!" shrilled a high-pitched female voice on the other side of the door.

He closed his eyes and the bed spun. Again his stomach heaved. O Christ, no! The sheets were clean, and they were white . . .

In the other room the recorded saxophone recommenced its plaintive appeal.

THE PARK

by James Matthews

HE LOOKED LONGINGLY at the children on the other side of the railings, the children sliding down the chute, landing with feet astride on the bouncy lawn; screaming as they almost touched the sky with each upward curve of their swings; their joyful, demented shrieks at each dip of the merry-go-round. He looked at them and his body trembled and itched to share their joy—buttocks to fit board, and hands and feet to touch steel. Next to him, on the ground, was a bundle of clothing, washed and ironed, wrapped in a sheet.

Five small boys, pursued by two bigger ones ran past, ignoring him. One of the bigger boys stopped. "What are you looking at, you brown ape?" the boy said, stooping to pick up a lump of clay. He recognized him. The boy had been present the day he was put out of the park. The boy pitched the lump, shattering it on the rail above his head, and the fragments fell onto his face.

He spat out the particles of clay clinging to the lining of his lips, eyes searching for an object to throw at the boys separated from him by the railings. More boys joined the one in front of him, and he was frightened by their number.

Without a word he shook his bundle free from the clay, raised it to his head, and walked away.

As he walked he recalled his last visit to the park. Without hesitation he had gone through the gates and got onto the nearest swing. Even now he could feel that pleasurable thrill that traveled the length of his body as he rocketed himself higher, higher, until he felt that the swing would upend him when it reached its peak. Almost leisurely he had allowed it to come to a halt, like a pendulum shortening its stroke, and then run toward the seesaw. A white boy, about his own age, was seated opposite him. Accordian-like, their legs folded to send the seesaw jerking from the indentation it pounded in the grass. A hand pressing on his shoulder stopped a jerk. He turned around to look into the face of the attendant.

"Get off!"

The skin tightened between his eyes. "Why must I get off? What have I done?" He held on, hands clamped onto the iron hoop attached to the wooden seesaw.

The white boy jumped off from the other end and stood, a detached spectator.

"You must get off!" The attendant spoke in a low voice so that it would not carry to the people who were gathering. "The Council says," he continued, "that we coloreds must not use the same swings as the whites. You must use the park where you stay." His voice apologizing for the uniform he wore that gave him the right to be in the park to watch that little whites were not hurt while playing.

"There's no park where we stay." He waved a hand in the direction of a block of flats. "There's a park on the other side of town, but I don't know where it is." He walked past them. The mothers with their babies, pink and belching, cradled in their arms, the children lolling on the grass, his companion from the seesaw, the nurse girls—their uniforms their badges of indemnity—pushing prams. Beside him walked the attendant.

At the entrance, the attendant pointed an accusing finger at a notice board. "There, you can read for yourself." Absolving himself of any blame.

He struggled with the red letters on the white background. *"Blankes Alleen,* Whites Only." He walked through the gates and behind him the swings screeched, the seesaw rattled, and the merry-go-round rumbled.

He walked past the park as on each occasion after that he had been forced to walk past it.

He shifted the bundle to a more comfortable position,

easing the pain biting into his shoulder muscles. What harm would I be doing if I were to use the swings? Would it stop the swings from swinging? Would the chute collapse? The bundle pressed deeper and the pain became an even line across his shoulders and he had no answer to his reasoning.

The park itself, with its wide lawns and flower beds and rockeries and dwarf trees, meant nothing to him. It was the gaily painted red-and-green tubing, the silver chains and brown boards, transport to never-never land, which gripped him.

Only once, long ago, and then almost as if by mistake, had he been on something to beat it. He had been taken by his father, one of those rare times when he was taken anywhere, to a fairground. He had stood captivated by the wooden horses with their gilded reins and scarlet saddles dipping in time to the music as they whirled by.

For a brief moment he was astride one, and he prayed it would last forever, but the moment lasted only the time it took him to whisper the prayer. Then he was standing, clutching his father's trousers, watching the other riders astride the dipping horses.

Another shifting of the bundle and he was at the house where he delivered the clothing his mother had washed in a round tub filled with boiling water, the steam covering her face with a film of sweat. Her voice, when she spoke, was as soft and clinging as the steam enveloping her.

He pushed the gate open and walked around the back, watching for the aged lap dog, which, at his entry, would rush out to wheeze asthmatically around his feet and nip with blunt teeth at his ankles.

A round-faced African girl, her blackness heightened by the white, starched uniform she wore, opened the kitchen door to let him in. She cleared the table and he placed the bundle on it.

"I will call madam," she said, the words spaced and highly pitched, as if she had some difficulty in uttering the syllables in English. Her buttocks bounced beneath the tight uniform and the backs of her calves shone with fat.

"Are you sure you've brought everything?" was the greeting he received each time he brought the bundle, and each time she checked every item and as usual nothing was missing. He looked at her and lowered his voice as he said, "Everything's there, madam."

What followed had become a routine between the three of them.

"Have you had anything to eat?" she asked him.

He shook his head.

"Well, we can't let you go off like that." Turning to the African woman in the white, starched uniform, "What have we got?"

The maid swung open the refrigerator door and took out a plate of food. She placed it on the table and set a glass of milk next to it.

When he was seated, the white woman left the kitchen and he was alone with the maid.

His nervousness left him and he could concentrate on what was on the plate.

A handful of peas, a dab of mashed potato, a tomato sliced into bleeding circles, a sprinkling of grated carrots, and no rice.

White people are funny, he told himself. How can anyone fill himself with this? It doesn't form a lump, like the food my mama makes.

He washed it down with milk.

"Thank you, Annie," he said as he pushed the glass aside.

Her teeth gleamed porcelain-white as she smiled.

He sat fidgeting, impatient to be outside, away from the kitchen with its glossy, tiled floor and steel cupboards Duco-ed a clinical white to match the food-stacked refrigerator.

"I see you have finished." The voice startled him. She held out an envelope containing the ten-shilling note—payment for his mother's weekly struggle over the wash tub. "This is for you." A sixpence was dropped into his hand, a long fingernail raking his palm.

"Thank you, madam." His voice barely audible.

"Tell your mother I'm going away on holiday for about a month and I will let her know when I'm back."

Then he was dismissed and her high heels tapped out of the kitchen.

He nodded his head at the African maid, who took an apple from a bowl that was bursting with fruit, and handed it to him.

Her smile bathed her face in light.

As he walked down the path he finished the apple with big bites.

Before he reached the gate the dog was after him, its hot breath warming his heels. He turned and poked his toes into its face. It barked hoarsely in protest, a look of outrage on its face.

He laughed delightedly at the expression, which changed the dog's features into those of an old man.

"Let's see you do that again." He waved his foot in front of the pug nose. The nose retreated and made an about-turn, waddling away with its dignity deflated by his affront.

As he walked, he mentally spent his sixpence.

I'll buy a penny drops, the sour ones which taste like limes, a penny bull's-eyes, a packet of sherbet with the licorice tube at the end of the packet, and a penny star toffees, red ones, which color your tongue and turn your spittle into blood.

His glands were titillated and his mouth filled with saliva. He stopped at the first shop and walked inside.

Trays were filled with expensive chocolates and sweets of a type never seen in the jars on the shelves of the Indian shop at the corner where he stayed. He walked out, not buying a thing.

His footsteps lagged as he reached the park.

The nurse girls with their babies and prams were gone, their places occupied by old men, who, with their hands holding up their stomachs, were casting disapproving eyes over the confusion and clatter confronting them.

A ball was kicked perilously close to one old man, and the boy who ran after it stopped as the old man raised his stick, daring him to come closer.

The rest of them called to the boy to get the ball. He edged closer and made a grab at it as the old man swung his cane. The cane missed him by more than a foot and he swaggered back, the ball held under his arm. Their game was resumed.

From the other side of the railings he watched them— the boys kicking the ball, the children cavorting on the grass, even the old men, senile on the seats; but most of all, the children enjoying themselves with what was denied him, and his whole body yearned to be part of them.

"Shit it!" He looked over his shoulder to see if anyone had heard him. "Shit it!" he said louder. "Shit on them! Their park, the grass, the swings, the seesaw. Everything! Shit it! Shit it!"

His small hands impotently shook the tall railings towering above his head.

It struck him that he would not be seeing the park for a whole month, that there would be no reason for him to pass it.

Despair filled him. He had to do something to ease his anger.

A bag filled with fruit peelings was on top of the rubbish stacked in a waste basket fitted to a pole. He reached for it and frantically threw it over the railings. He ran without waiting to see the result.

Out of breath three streets farther, he slowed down, pain stabbing beneath his heart. The act had brought no relief, only intensified the longing.

He was oblivious of the people passing, the hoots of the vehicles whose path he crossed without thinking. And once, when he was roughly pushed aside, he did not even bother to look and see who had done it.

The familiar shrieks and smells told him he was home.

The Indian shop could not draw him out of his melancholy mood and he walked past it, his sixpence unspent, in his pocket.

A group of boys were playing with tires on the pavement.

Some of them called to him but he ignored them and turned into a short side street.

He mounted the flat stoep of a two-story house with a façade that must have been painted once but had now turned a nondescript gray with the red brick underneath showing through.

Beyond the threshold the room was dim. He walked past the scattered furniture with a familiarity that did not need guidance.

His mother was in the kitchen, hovering above a pot perched on a pressure stove.

He placed the envelope on the table. She put aside the spoon and stuck a finger under the flap of the envelope, tearing it in half. She placed the ten shilling note in a spoutless teapot on the shelf.

"Are you hungry?"

He nodded his head.

She poured him a cup of soup and added a thick slice of brown bread.

Between bites of bread and sips of the soup, which scalded his throat, he told her that there wouldn't be any washing coming during the week.

"Why? What's the matter? What have I done?"

"Nothing. Madam said she's going away for a month and she'll let Mama know when she gets back."

"What am I going to do now?" Her voice took on a whine and her eyes strayed to the teapot containing the money. The whine hardened to reproach as she continued. "Why didn't she let me know she was going away? I could have looked for another madam."

She paused. "I slave away and the pain never leaves my back, and it's too much for her to let me know she's going away. The money I get from her just keeps us nicely steady. How am I going to cover the hole?"

As he ate, he wondered how the ten shillings he had brought helped to keep them nicely steady. There was no change in their meals. It was, as usual, not enough, and the only time they received new clothes was at Christmas.

"There's the burial to pay and I was going to ask Mr. Lemonsky to bring some lino for the front room. I'm sick of seeing boards where the lino's worn through, but it's no use asking him to bring it now. Without money you have as much hope as getting wine on a Saturday."

He hurried his eating to get away from the words wafting toward him, before they could soak into him, trapping him in the chair to witness his mother's miseries.

Outside, they were still playing with their tires. He joined them half-heartedly. As he rolled the tire his spirit was in the park on the swings. There was no barrier to his coming and he could do as he pleased. He was away from the narrow streets and squawking children and speeding cars. He was in a place of green grass and red tubing and silver steel. The tire rolled past him. He made no effort to grab it.

"Go get the tire." "Are you asleep?" "Don't you want to play any more?" He walked away, ignoring their cries.

Rage boiled up inside him. Rage against the houses with their streaked walls and smashed panes filled by too many people; against the overflowing garbage pails outside doors, the alleys and streets; and against a law he could not understand—a law that shut him out of the park.

He burst into tears. He swept his arms across his cheeks to check his weeping.

He lowered his hands to peer at the boy confronting him.

"I'm not crying, damn you. Something's gone into my eye and I was rubbing it."

"I think you're crying."

He pushed past and continued toward the shop. "Crying doll!" The boy's taunt rang after him.

The shop's sole, iron-barred window was crowded. Oranges were mixed with writing paper and dried figs were strewn on school slates; clothing and crockery collected dust. Across the window a cockroach made its leisurely way, antennae on the alert.

Inside the shop was as crowded as the window. Bags covered the floor, leaving a narrow path to the counter.

The shopkeeper, an ancient Indian with a face tanned like cracked leather, leaned across the counter. "Yes, boy?" He showed teeth scarlet with betel. "C'mon, boy. What you want? No stand here all day." His jaws worked at the betel nut held captive by his stained teeth.

He ordered penny portions of his selections.

Transferring the sweets to his pocket, he threw the torn container on the floor and walked out. Behind him the Indian murmured grimly, jaws working faster.

One side of the street was in shadow. He sat with his back against the wall, savoring the last of the sun.

Bull's-eye, peppermint, a piece of licorice—all lumped

together in his cheek. For a moment, the park was forgotten.

He watched the girl advancing without interest.

"Mama says you must come 'n' eat." She stared at his bulging cheek, one hand rubbing the side of her nose. "Gimme." He gave her a bull's-eye, which she dropped into her mouth between dabs at her nose.

"Wipe your snot!" he ordered her, showing his superiority. He walked past. She followed, sucking and sniffing.

When they entered the kitchen their father was already seated at the table.

"Why must I always send somebody after you?" his mother said.

He slipped into his seat and then hurriedly got up to wash his hands before his mother could find fault with yet another point.

Supper was a silent affair except for the scraping of spoon across plate and an occasional sniff from his sister.

Almost at the end of the meal a thought came to mind. He sat, spoon poised in the air, shaken by its magnitude. Why not go to the park after dark? After it had closed its gates on the old men, the children, and nurses with their prams! There would be no one to stop him.

He couldn't think further. He was lightheaded with the thought of it. His mother's voice, as she related her day to his father, was not the steam that stung but a soft breeze wafting past him, leaving him undisturbed.

Then qualms troubled him. He had never been in that part of town at night. A band of fear tightened across his chest, contracting his insides, making it hard for him to swallow his food. He gripped his spoon more tightly, stretching the skin across his knuckles.

I'll do it! I'll go to the park as soon as we're finished eating. He controlled himself with difficulty. He swallowed what was left on his plate and furtively checked to see how the others were faring. Hurry it up! Hurry it up!

When his father pushed the last plate aside and lit a cigarette, he hastily cleared the table and began washing up.

Each piece of crockery washed, he passed on to his sister, whose sniffing kept pace with their combined operation.

The dishes done, he swept the kitchen and carried out the garbage bin.

"Can I go out and play, Mama?"

"Don't let me have to send for you again."

His father remained silent, buried behind his newspaper.

"Before you go"—his mother stopped him—"light the lamp and hang it in the passage."

He filled the lamp with paraffin, turned up its wick and lit it. The light glimmered weakly through the streaked glass.

The moon to him was a fluorescent ball—light without

warmth—and the stars, fragments chipped off it. Beneath street lights card games were in session. As he walked past, he sniffed the nostril-prickling smell of dagga. Dim doorways could not conceal couples clutching at each other.

Once clear of the district he broke into a jog-trot. He did not slacken his pace as he passed through downtown with its wonderland shopwindows. As he neared the park his elation seeped out and his footsteps dragged.

In front of him was the park with its gate and iron railings. Behind the railings stood, impaled, the notice board. He could see the swings beyond. The sight strengthened him.

He walked over, his breath coming faster. There was no one in sight. A car turned the corner and came toward him, and he started at the sound of its engine. The car swept past, the tires softly licking the asphalt.

The railings were icy cold to his touch, and the shock sent him into action. Extending his arms, with monkeylike movements he pulled himself up to perch on top of the railings, then dropped on the newly turned earth.

The grass was damp with dew, and he swept his feet across it. Then he ran, and the wet grass bowed beneath his bare feet.

He ran from the swings to the merry-go-round, seesaw to chute, hands covering the metal.

Up the steps to the top of the chute. He stood outlined against the sky. He was a bird, an eagle. He flung himself down on his stomach, sliding swiftly. *Wheeeeeeee!* He rolled over when he slammed onto the grass. He was looking at the moon for an instant, then propelled himself to his feet and ran for the steps of the chute to recapture that feeling of flight. Each time he swept down the chute he wanted the trip never to end, to go on sliding, sliding, sliding.

He walked reluctantly past the seesaw, consoling himself with pushing at one end to send it whacking on the grass.

"Shit it!" He grunted as he strained to set the merry-go-round in motion. Thigh tensed, leg stretched, he pushed. The merry-go-round moved. He increased his exertion and jumped on, one leg trailing at the ready, to shove if it should slow down. The merry-go-round dipped and swayed. To keep it moving, he had to push more than he rode. Not wanting to spoil his pleasure he jumped off and raced for the swings.

Feet astride, hands clutching silver chains, he jerked his body to gain momentum. He crouched like a runner, then violently straightened. The swing widened its arc. It swept higher, higher, higher. It reached the sky. He could touch the moon. He plucked a star to pin to his breast. The earth was far below him. No bird could fly as high as he. Upward and onward he went.

A light switched on in the hut at the far side of the park. It was a small patch of yellow on a dark square. The door opened and he saw a dark figure in the doorway.

Then the door was shut and the figure strode toward him. He knew it was the attendant. A torch glinted brightly in the moonlight as it swung at his side.

He continued swinging.

The attendant came to a halt in front of him, out of reach of the swing's arc, and flashed his torch. The light caught him in mid-air.

"God dammit!" the attendant swore. "I've told you before you can't get on the swings."

The rattle of chains when the boy shifted his feet was the only answer he received.

"Why did you come back?"

"The swings. I came back for the swings."

The attendant catalogued the things denied them because of their color. Even his job depended on their good will.

"Blerry whites! They got everything."

All his feelings urged him to leave the boy alone, to let him continue to enjoy himself. But the fear that someone might see them hardened him.

"Get off! Go home!" he screamed, his voice harsh, his anger directed at the system that drove him against his own. "If you don't get off, I'll go for the police. You know what they'll do to you."

The swing raced back and forth.

The attendant turned and raced toward the gate.

"Mama. Mama." His lips trembled, wishing himself safe in his mother's kitchen sitting next to the still-burning stove with a comic spread across his knees. "Mama. Mama!" His voice mounted, wrenching from his throat, keeping pace with the soaring swing as it climbed to the sky. Voice and swing. Swing and voice. Higher. Higher. Higher. Until they were one.

At the entrance to the park the notice board stood tall, its shadow elongated, pointing toward him.

RAIN

by Richard Rive

RAIN POURED DOWN, blotting out all sound with
its sharp and vibrant tattoo. Dripping neon signs reflect-
ing lurid reds and yellows in mirror-wet streets. Swollen
gutters. Water overflowing and squelching on to pavements. Gurgling and sucking at storm-water drains. Table
Mountain cut off by a gray film of mist and rain. A lost
City Hall clock trying manfully to chime nine over an
indifferent Cape Town. Baleful reverberations through
a spluttering all-consuming drizzle.

Yellow light filters through from Solly's "Grand Fish
and Chips Palace." Door tight-shut against the weather.
Inside stuffy with heat, hot bodies, steaming clothes, and
the nauseating smell of stale fish oil. Misty patterns on
the plate-glass windows and a messy pool where rain has

filtered beneath the door and mixed with the sawdust.

Solly himself in shirt sleeves, sweating, vulgar, and moody. Bellowing at a dripping woman who has just come in.

"Shut 'e damn door. Think you live in a tent?"

"Ag, Solly."

"Don' ag me. You colored people can never shut blarry doors."

"Don't bloomingwell swear at me."

"I bloomingwell swear at you, yes."

"Come. Gimme two pieces 'e fish. Tail cut."

"Two pieces 'e fish."

"Raining like hell outside," the woman said to no one.

"Mmmmmm. Raining like hell," a thin befezzed Malay cut in.

"One an' six. Thank you. An' close 'e door behin' you."

"Thanks. Think you got 'e on'y door in Hanover Street?"

"Go to hell!" Solly cut the conversation short and turned to another customer.

The northwester sobbed heavy rain squalls against the windowpanes. The Hanover Street bus screeched to a slithery stop and passengers darted for shelter in a cinema entrance. The street lamps shone blurredly.

Solly sweated as he wrapped parcels of fish and chips in a newspaper. Fish and chips. Vinegar? Wrap? One an' six please. Thank you! Next. Fish and chips. No?

Two fish. No chips? Salt? Vinegar? One an' six please. Thank you! Next. Fish an' chips.

"Close 'e blarry door!" Solly glared daggers at a woman who had just come in. She half smiled apologetically at him.

"You colored people are worse than Kaffirs."

She struggled with the door and then stood dripping in a pool of wet sawdust. Solly left the counter to add two presto logs to the furnace. She moved out of the way. Another customer showed indignation at Solly's remark.

"You blooming Jews are always making colored people out."

"Go to hell!" Solly dismissed the attack on his race. Fish an' chips. Vinegar? Salt? One an' six. Thank you.

"Yes, madam?"

"Could you tell me when the bioscope comes out?"

"Am I the blooming manager?"

"Please."

"Half pas' ten," the Malay offered helpfully.

"Thank you. Can I stay here till then? It's raining outside."

"I know it's blarrywell raining, but this is not a Salvation Army."

"Please, baas!"

This caught Solly unawares. He had had his shop in that corner of District Six since most could remember and had been called a great many unsavory things in the

211

years. Solly didn't mind. But this caught him unawares. Please, baas. This felt good. His imagination adjusted a black bow tie to an evening suit. Please, baas.

"Okay, stay for a short while. But then 'e rain stops you go!" She nodded dumbly and tried to make out the blurred name of the cinema opposite, through the misted windows.

"Waitin' for somebody?" Solly asked. No response.

"I ask if yer waitin' fer somebody!" The figure continued to stare.

"Oh go to hell," said Solly, turning to another customer.

Through the rain blur Siena stared at nothing in particular. Dim visions of slippery wet cars. Honking and wheezing in the rain. Spluttering buses. Heavy, drowsy voices in the Grand Fish and Chips Palace. Her eyes traveled beyond the street and the water cascades of Table Mountain, beyond the winter of Cape Town to the summer of the Boland. Past the green grapelands of Stellenbosch and Paarl and the stuffy wheat district of Malmesbury to the lazy sun and laughter of Teslaarsdal. A tired sun here. An uninterested sun. Now it seemed that the sun was weary of the physical effort of having to rise, to shine, to comfort, and to set.

Inside the nineteenth-century, gabled mission church she had first met Joseph. The church is still there, and beautiful, and the ivy climbs over it and makes it more beautiful. Huge silver oil lamps suspended from the roof, polished and shining. It was in the flicker of the lamps that she had first become aware of him. He was visiting

from Cape Town. She sang that night like she had never
sung before. Her favorite psalm.

"All ging ik ook in een dal der schaduw des doods
. . . Though I walk through the valley of the shadow
of death . . . der schaduw des doods." And then he had
looked at her. Everyone had looked at her, for she was
good in solos.

"Ik zoude geen kwaad vreezen . . . I will fear no evil."
And she had not feared, but loved. Had loved him.
Had sung for him. For the wide eyes, the yellow skin,
the high cheekbones. She had sung for a creator who
could create a man like Joseph. "Want gij zijt met mij;
Uw stok en Uw staf, die vertroosten mij."

Those were black and white polka-dot nights when the
moon did a golliwogg cakewalk across a banjo-strung sky.
Nights of sweet remembrances when he had whispered
love to her and told her of Cape Town. She had giggled
coyly at his obscenities. It was fashionable, she hoped,
to giggle coyly at obscenities. He lived in one of those
streets off District Six and was, he boasted, quite a one
amongst the girls. She heard of Molly and Miena and
Sophia and a sophisticated Charmaine, who was almost
a schoolteacher and always spoke English. But he told
her that he had only found love in Teslaarsdal. She wasn't
sure whether to believe him. And then he had felt her
richness and the moon darted behind a cloud.

The loud screeching of the train to Cape Town. Screeching loud enough to drown the protest of her family.
The wrath of her father. The icy stares of Teslaarsdal

matrons. Loud and confused screechings to drown her hysteria, her ecstasy. Drowned and confused in the roar of a thousand cars and a hundred thousand lights and a summer of carnival evenings that is Cape Town. Passion in a tiny room off District Six. Desire surrounded by four bare walls and a rickety chair and a mounted cardboard tract that murmured *Bless this House*.

And the agony of the nights when he came home later and later and sometimes not at all. The waning of his passion and whispered names of others. Molly and Miena and Sophia. Charmaine. The helpless knowledge that he was slipping from her. Faster and faster. Gathering momentum.

"Not that I'm saying so but I only heard . . ."

"Why don't you go to bioscope one night and see for yourself . . ."

"Marian's man is searching for Joseph . . ." Searching for Joseph. Looking for Joseph. Knifing for Joseph. Joseph. Joseph! JOSEPH! Molly! Miena! Sophia! Names! Names! Names! Gossip. One-sided desire. Go to bioscope and see. See what? See why? When! When!

And after he had been away a week she decided to see. Decided to go through the rain and stand in a sweating fish and chips shop owned by a blaspheming Jew. And wait for the cinema to come out.

The rain had stopped sobbing against the plate-glass window. A skin-soaking drizzle now set in. Continuous. Unending. Filming everything with dark depression. A shivering, weeping neon sign flickered convulsively on and off. A tired Solly shot a quick glance at a cheap alarm clock.

"Half pas' ten, bioscope out soon."

Siena looked more intently through the misty screen. No movement whatsoever in the deserted cinema foyer.

"Time it was bloomingwell out." Solly braced himself for the wave of after-show customers who would invade his Palace.

"Comin' out late tonight, missus."

"Thank you, baas."

Solly rubbed sweat out of his eyes and took in her neat and plain figure. Tired face but good legs. A few late stragglers catching colds in the streets. Wet and squally outside.

"Your man in bioscope?"

She was intent on a khaki-uniformed usher struggling to open the door.

"Man in bioscope, missus?"

The cinema had to come out some time or other. An usher opening the door, adjusting the outside gate. Preparing for the crowds to pour out. Vomited and spilled out.

"Man in bioscope?"

No response.

"Oh, go to hell!"

They would be out now. Joseph would be out. She rushed for the door, throwing words of thanks to Solly.

"Close the blarry door!"

She never heard him. The drizzle had stopped. An

unnatural calm hung over the empty foyer, over the deserted street. Over her empty heart. She took up her stand on the bottom step. Expectantly. Her heart pounding.

Then they came. Pouring, laughing, pushing, jostling. She stared with fierce intensity, but faces passed too fast. Laughing, roaring, gay. Wide-eyed, yellow-skinned, high-cheekboned. Black, brown, ivory, yellow. Black-eyed, laughing-eyed, gay, bouncing. No Joseph. Palpitating heart that felt like bursting into a thousand pieces. If she should miss him. She found herself searching for the wrong face. Solly's face. Ridiculously searching for hard blue eyes and a sharp white chin in a sea of ebony and brown. Solly's face. Missing half a hundred faces and then again searching for the familiar high cheekbones. Solly. Joseph. Molly. Miena. Charmaine.

The drizzle restarted. Studying overcoats instead of faces. Longing for the pale blue shirt she had seen in the shop at Solitaire. A bargain at £1.5s. She had scraped and scrounged to buy it for him. A week's wages. Collecting her thoughts and continuing the search for Joseph. And then the thinning out of the crowd and the last few stragglers. The ushers shutting the iron gates. They might be shutting Joseph in. Herself out. Only the ushers left. And the uncompromising iron gates.

"Please, is Joseph inside?"

"Who's Joseph?"

"Is Joseph still inside?"

"Joseph who?"

They were teasing her. Laughing behind her back. Preventing her from finding him.

"Joseph is inside!" she shouted frenziedly.

"Look, merrim, it's raining cats an' dogs. Go home."

Go home. To whom? To what? An empty room? An empty bed? A tract that shrieked its lie, *Bless this House?*

And then she was aware of the crowd on the corner. Maybe he was there. Running and peering into every face. Joseph. The crowd in the drizzle. Two battling figures. Joseph. Figures locked in struggle slithering in the wet gutter. Muck streaking down clothes through which wet bodies were silhouetted. Joseph. A blue shirt. And then she wiped the rain out of her eyes and saw him. Fighting for his life. Desperately kicking in the gutter. Joseph. The blast of a police whistle. A pickup van screeching to a stop.

"Please, sir, it wasn't him. They all ran away. Please, sir, he's Joseph. He done nothing. He done nothing, my baas. Please sir, he's my Joseph. Please, baas!"

"Maak dat jy weg kom. Get away. Voetsak!"

"Please, sir, it wasn't him. They ran away!"

Alone. An empty bed. An empty room.

Solly's Grand Fish and Chips Palace crowded out. People milling inside. Rain once more squalling and sobbing against the door and windows. Swollen gutters unable to cope with the giddy rush of water. Solly sweating to deal with the after-cinema rush.

Fish an' chips. Vinegar? Salt? One an' six. Thank you. Sorry, no fish. Wait five minutes. Chips on'y. Vinegar?

Ninepence. Tickey change. Thank you. Sorry, no fish.
Five minutes' time. Chips? Ninepence. Thank you. Solly
paused for breath and stirred the fish.

"What's 'e trouble outside?"

"Bioscope, Solly."

"No, man, outside!"

"I say, bioscope."

"What were 'e police doin'? Sorry, no fish yet, sir.
Five minutes' time. What were 'e police doin'?"

"A fight in 'e blooming rain."

"Jeeesus, in 'e rain?"

"Ja."

"Who was fightin'?"

"Joseph an' somebody."

"Joseph?"

"Ja, fellow in Arundel Street."

"Yes, I know Joseph. Always in trouble. Chucked him
outta here a'reddy."

"Well, that chap."

"An' who?"

"Dinno."

"Police get them?"

"Got Joseph."

"Why were 'ey fightin'? Fish in a minute, sir."

"Over a dame."

"Who?"

"You know Miena who works by Patel? Now she. Her
boyfriend caught 'em."

"In bioscope?"

"Ja."

Solly chuckled deeply, suggestively.

"See that woman an 'e police?"

"What woman?"

"Dame cryin' to 'e police."

"They say it's Joseph's dame."

"Joseph always got plenty 'e dames. F-I-S-H—
R-E-A-D-Y! ! ! Two pieces for you, sir? One an' six.
Shilling change. Fish an' chips? One an' six. Thank you.
Fish on'y? Vinegar? Salt? Ninepence. Tickey change.
Thank you!"

"What you say about 'e woman?"

"They say Joseph's girl was crying to 'e police."

"Oh, he got plenty 'e girls."

"This one was living with him."

"Oh, what she look like? Fish, sir?"

"Okay. Nice legs."

"Hmmmmm," said Solly, "Hey, close 'e damn door.
Oh, you again." Siena came in. A momentary silence.
Then a buzzing and whispering.

"Oh," said Solly, nodding as someone whispered over
the counter to him, "I see. She was waiting here. Musta
been waitin' for him." A young girl in jeans giggled.

"Fish an' chips costs one an' six, madam."

"Wasn't it one an' three before?"

"Before the Boer war, madam. Price of fish go up.

Potatoes go up an' you expect me to charge one an'
three?"

"Why not?"

"Oh, go to hell! Next, please!"

"Yes, that's 'e one Solly."

"Mmmm. Excuse me, madam"—turning to Siena—"like
some fish an' chips? Free of charge, never min' 'e money."

"Thank you, my baas."

The rain now sobbed wildly as the shop emptied, and
Solly counted the cash in his till. Thousands of watery
horses charging down the street. Rain drilling into cobbles
and pavings. Miniature waterfalls down the sides of
buildings. Blurred lights through unending streams. Siena
listlessly holding the newspaper parcel of fish and chips.

"You can stay here till it clears up," said Solly.

She looked up tearfully.

Solly grinned, showing his yellow teeth. "It's quite
okay."

A smile flickered across her face for a second.

"It's quite okay by me."

She looked down and hesitated for a moment. Then
she struggled against the door. It yielded with a crash
and the northwester howled into Solly's Palace.

"Close 'e blarry door!" he said, grinning.

"Thank you, my baas," she said as she shivered out
into the rain.

BIOGRAPHICAL
NOTES

𝕾𝕰𝕺𝕮𝕰𝕺𝕮𝕰𝕺𝕮𝕰𝕺𝕮𝕰𝕺𝕮𝕰𝕺𝕮𝕰𝕺𝕮𝕰𝕺𝕮

RICHARD RIVE—was born in Cape Town in 1931, and
was educated at Trafalgar High School, Hewat Training
College (where he qualified as a teacher), and at the
University of Cape Town. He now teaches English and
Latin at a high school in Cape Town. His collection of
short stories *African Songs* has appeared in English and
Swedish. It contains many prize-winning and best-recom-
mended stories. His first novel, *Emergency,* is soon to be
published. In March, 1962, he was awarded a Fairfield
Foundation Fellowship to travel and study literary
trends in Africa and Europe. He has been published in
South Africa *(Fighting Talk, New Age, Drum, Groote*

Schuur, Contrast), United States of America *(African Treasury, New York Post, Negro Digest, Peaceful Heroes)*, Great Britain *(Darkness and Light)*, Italy *(Almanacco Literrario)*, Austria *(Der Krystal)*, Sweden *(Afrika Berattar)*, Germany *(Atlantis, Seven Seas)*, Finland *(Afrika Kertoo)*, and Ghana *(School Anthology)*.

ALEX LA GUMA—was born in Cape Town in 1925, and attended high school. He worked as clerk, factory hand, messenger, bookkeeper, photographer, and journalist. He studied painting for a short time, then turned to writing. He worked for a Cape Town newspaper as reporter and columnist. He has been published in South Africa *(Fighting Talk, Drum, Africa South)*, Brazil, Sweden *(Afrika Berattar)*, and Finland *(Afrika Kertoo)*. His first novel, *Walk in the Night*, was acclaimed at the Mbari writers' conference held in Kampala. The novel was published by Mbari and then by Andre Deutsch. One of the 156 accused in the South African treason trial, which started in 1956, he was acquitted three years later. He was detained in prison for five months during the 1960 state of emergency. Now banned from attending any gathering in the Republic of South Africa and South West Africa, he is confined to two magisterial districts in the Cape Peninsula. None of his utterances or writings may be reproduced or distributed in South Africa.

JAMES MATTHEWS—was born in Cape Town in 1929,

the eldest son of a large poor family. His first job was selling newspapers while still at school. After leaving high school, he was in turn a messenger, a journalist on *Drum*, and is at present a receptionist. His collection of short stories, *Azikwelwa*, has just been published in Swedish. He has also completed a novel, which is in the hands of his publishers. He has been published in South Africa *(Africa South, Drum, Cape Times* and *Cape Argus)*, Sweden *(Afrika Berattar)*, and Finland *(Afrika Kertoo)*.

ALF WANNENBURGH—was born in Cape Town in 1936. Matriculated in 1953, he attended University of Cape Town. He worked as land-surveyor's assistant, salesman, clerk, and window dresser. His first writings were political articles for local journals and the *Tribune* (London). He also wrote commercial short stories for trade publications. He then changed to writing serious short stories, and has been published in South Africa *(Fighting Talk, New Age, New African,* and *Adelphi Literary Review)*, United States of America *(Negro Digest)*, Ghana *(School Anthology)*, and Germany *(Atlantis)*.